Political Family

by

Heather Dawn Thoroman

authorHOUSE™

1663 LIBERTY DRIVE, SUITE 200
BLOOMINGTON, INDIANA 47403
(800) 839-8640
WWW.AUTHORHOUSE.COM

© 2004 Heather Dawn Thoroman
All Rights Reserved.

No part of this book may be reproduced, stored in a retrieval system, or transmitted by any means without the written permission of the author.

First published by AuthorHouse 10/11/04

ISBN: 1-4208-0438-3 (sc)

Library of Congress Control Number: 2004098033

Printed in the United States of America
Bloomington, Indiana

This book is printed on acid-free paper.

Chapter One

Travis Moore hung the phone up and tapped his long fingers on the receiver. "What did Steve and Brad have to say?" asked his wife Jessica. He turned around and looked at her. He had almost forgotten that she was there. "Well, don't keep me in suspense. What did they say?"

Travis met her wide set green eyes and gave her a smile. "They probably want to know if I'll be running for the Senate again. They are going to meet me at my office." He put his black suite jacket on and straightened the collar on it. "Remember that Clark and Jeffery are going to retire after this term." He picked up the brush and ran it through his salt and pepper hair.

"I remember."

"And this is also President Chandler's last term in office as well. With a year and a half to the election they are trying to keep as many democrats as they can in office."

Jessica gave him a smile. Travis was a popular senator from Montana, well liked and respected by both the republicans and democrats. Before becoming a senator, Travis had been a successful defense attorney. "They'll be happy to know that you are going to run again." She

1

brushed her shoulder length auburn hair out of her face. Her green eyes filled with concern.

Travis saw the change and sat down on the bed next to her. "What's wrong?"

"Abby is not going to be happy about this. She has never liked living in the lime light."

Travis sighed. He knew that she was right. Their only child, sixteen year old, Abby, had never liked the fact that she had been forced to move across the country leaving behind her friends. She was less happy about being forced into the public eye. On more than one occasion she had skipped an important function. "She has resented me because I disrupted her life."

We have drifted apart in the last four years, he thought to himself sadly. *I don't even know how to make things better between us.*

Jessica put a hand on his arm and gave it a gentle squeeze. She knew that he was upset over his estrangement from Abby. "You need to talk to her, Travis," she advised him.

He looked out the window of their bedroom and watched a robin land on the tree next to their house. Travis looked back at Jessica. "I don't know how to talk to her anymore. All we ever do is argue."

"You have to talk to her, Travis! You can't let your relationship with her continue to fall apart."

"How do you suggest that I do that? I am trying to make things better between the two of us."

"You are not trying hard enough," she snapped at him. Jessica got up from the bed and picked her bathrobe and wrapped it around her. "You have to keep working at it, Travis," she said softly. "If you don't keep trying we are going to lose our daughter."

He blinked back tears and checked his watch. If he did not leave soon he would be late for his meeting. "I have to go." He walked out of their bedroom and went down the stairs. Jessica was right behind him. "I am going to late for my meeting."

"What about Abby?"

"I'll talk to her when I get home."

"Travis!"

He turned around and glared at her. "I know that I need to talk to her and I will."

Jessica folded her arms across her chest and gave him an equally icy glare of her own. "Famous last words."

Travis ignored her last comment and marched out of the front door. Jessica went into the living room and sat down on the leather couch. She was seething with anger and frustration. *He won't talk to her,* she thought to herself, *I know he won't talk to her. He'll leave it me to do all the dirty work.*

She had been the one to tell their daughter that Travis was going to run for the Senate. And when her father had won the election she was the one to tell Abby that they were moving from Sunset, Montana to Washington D.C.

"Morning Mom," Jessica heard Abby say from behind her. She turned around and looked at Abby. She was shocked at what her daughter had on. Abby was dressed in a short tight black skirt and a dark red halter-top. Her long auburn hung straight down to the middle of her back. "I heard you and Daddy dearest yelling at one another."

"Abby, really," admonished her mother. "do you have to dress like a slut?"

Abby laughed and smoothed her red hair. "Sure do. Michael likes it when I dress like this."

Jessica felt herself growing even more frustrated. "You are not to see that boy! Your father and I forbid it"

Abby laughed again. *Michael is about the only thing that you and Daddy do agree on,* Abby thought to herself. She pulled out her lipstick from the purse and added more to her lips making them look redder. "I am sixteen, you can't tell me who I can see and can't see."

"You live in my house and you will do what I say!"

Abby put the lipstick back into her purse and zipped it up. "You can't stop me from seeing him. And neither can dad." she headed toward the door.

Jessica stood up and hurried after Abby. "Come back here!" she ordered. But she knew it was hopeless as she watched Abby get into her black BMW and sped down the drive. She felt tears well up in her eyes and she went back into the house. She walked back into the living room and collapsed on to the recliner. *What's happening to this family,* she thought despondently. She buried her face in her hands and began to cry.

* * * * * * * * * * *

Travis waited for Brad and Steve at his office. He played with the American flag that was sitting on the corner of his desk. He knew he should be doing some paper work, but he could not make himself do it. The intercom beeped and he pushed the respond button. "Yes, Amy?"

"Senator Blackwell and Johnson are here to see you."

"Show them in."

"Yes, sir."

Travis stood up when they entered his office. He held out his hand to Brad first. "Hi, Brad how are you?"

"I am fine."

4

Travis then turned to Steve Blackwell and shook his hand as well. "Steve, it's great to see you again. How is your family?"

"Nice to see you again too, Senator. The family is fine. Jennifer will be home from college this weekend," Steve said, giving Travis a friendly smile.

Travis motioned for them to take the two chairs in front of his desk and they all sat down. "What can I do for you gentlemen?"

Brad Johnson, the older of the two senators, began to speak. "We have something important to discuss with you." He ran a hand through his pitch white hair.

Travis nodded his head. "This has something to do with the election doesn't it?"

Steve Blackwell scooted up in his chair. "Yes, it does. We assumed that you are going to run for the Senate again."

"I have been thinking about it," he admitted. "I probably will run again." *Abby and Jessica will not be happy about this,* he thought to himself. "I think I can still do a lot of good for the American people."

Steve nodded in agreement. He looked over at the older senator. "In fact that's what we want to talk to you about."

Travis's interest was peeked now. "About?"

Brad leaned closer to Travis. He had a twinkle in his dark brown eyes. "As you know this is President Chandler's last term in office. And we are going to need a new president come next November."

"I don't understand what that has to do with me."

"We want you to run for president," Brad said. "You are young, you have great ideas for this country and, you are popular with both parties. You are the perfect choice."

5

Travis sat back in his chair. "You want me to run for president?" he looked out the window. "I don't know what to say."

"Think about it, Travis. We want you be the democratic presidential nominee," Steve said.

Do I want to be president? "I'll have to talk to my family of course. This is going to be a big decision."

Both the senators stood up. "Of course," Brad said. "Talk it over with your family. But don't take to long because we need to start planning your campaign."

"I'll let you know by next week," Travis promised. He shook hands with both Brad and Steve again and they left the office. "President." he said with a smile. Travis reached over and picked up his phone and dialed his home number. He could not wait to tell Jessica.

"Hello?" the housekeeper Nancy answered. "This is the Moore residence."

"Hi, Nancy, it's Senator Moore. Is my wife home?"

"She is home, Senator Moore. But she is not feeling well."

Travis felt his heart drop. He knew that his wife had been having headaches lately. "Is it a migraine?" he asked, but he already knew the answer.

"I assume so, sir. She has had a heating pad on her forehead for about an hour. She told me that she did not want to be disturbed."

"Tell her I called," Travis told the housekeeper. "Tell her I hope that she feels better soon."

"I'll tell her, Senator. Is there anything else?" Nancy asked him.

"No, I'll see her at home soon. Bye, Nancy."

"Bye, Senator."

Travis hung up the phone. He knew that contemplating a run for the White House would put more stress on her. He picked up some papers and began reading through some of the proposals when his phone rang. He picked it up thinking it would be Jessica. "Hi, honey."

"Hello, sweetie," a voice answered him back. It was voice that he was used to, but not on the phone.

"President Chandler! I am sorry sir. I thought it would be my wife," he apologized.

President Chandler gave a hearty laugh. "That's alright Senator. I have heard rumors going around that you were running for president. I just wanted to see if they were true."

"Senators Blackwell and Johnson were at my office earlier today. They were trying to convince me to run."

"I hope you will consider it. I think you would make a great president for this country. You have done a great job handling foreign affairs," Chandler told him.

"Thank you, sir," he said, feeling pleased that the president thought so highly of him. "I will of course have to talk to my family about this."

"I hope you will run, Travis. And I want you to know that you will have my total support," President Chandler promised.

"Thank you, Mr. President. But as I have said before I need to talk to my family before deciding anything," Travis said.

"Of course," President Chandler said. "Let me know what you decide."

"I will, sir. And thank you again."

"Bye, Senator Moore."

"Goodbye, Mr. President." Travis hung up his phone. He got up from his chair and looked out the window.

President Moore, he thought to himself with a smile on his face. *Slow down Travis. Think about how this will affect your family.* He went back to his desk and touched the intercom. "Amy?"

"Yes, sir? Is there a problem?" she asked him.

"No. But, I do want you to cancel my appointments for the rest of the day. I need to go home. There are some important things that I need to discuss with Jessica."

"Okay, Senator," she said, and disconnected their connection.

Travis took his jacket that was hanging on the coat rack. Before he left he gave last minute instructions to Amy. Travis walked out to his blue Mercedes and climbed into it. He could not stop smiling. He felt like a little boy who had gotten a bicycle for Christmas. He drove through Washington D.C. till he got to the suburb that he lived in. He pulled his car into the circular drive in front of his red brick house. He got out of the car and ran up to the house. He flung the door open scaring Nancy who was in the living room dusting. "Sorry," he said, as he raced up the stairs two at a time. He reached his bedroom and opened the door. "Jessie!" he cried out excitedly. "I have great news."

She sat up slowly on the bed still holding the heating pad to her head. "What's going on?"

He sat down at the foot of the bed. "Guess what Steve Blackwell and Brad Johnson wanted to ask me."

She could see that he was really happy. Giddy. She shrugged her shoulders. "They want you to run for the Senate?"

"More than that."

She was not in the mood to play guessing games. She glared at him and adjusted her heating pad. "Just tell me."

Travis did not notice that his wife was in a foul mood. He was too excited to notice anything else but himself. "They want me to run for president!"

I must have heard him wrong, she thought, *he did not just say that they want him to run for president.* She stared at her husband in shock. "What did you say?"

"They want me to run for president! Isn't that exciting?"

Jessica tried to feel happy for Travis, but all she could feel was a sinking feeling in her gut. "That's what I thought you said."

"Isn't that exciting?" Travis got up from the bed. "When will Abby be home? I can't wait to tell her."

Jessica took the heating pad off her head and turned it off. "I don't think Abby will be happy about this."

Travis felt some of his happiness drain from him. "Are you happy for me?"

She stood up and put the heating pad on the desk. It was not going to help her anymore anyway. "Of course I am happy for you."

"Yes, I can tell."

She turned to look at him. "Travis, I am happy for you," she snapped at him. "But I am thinking about Abby and how she will feel about this." *You are not making this is any easier,* Jessica thought angrily. He was not thinking about how Abby would feel about all this.

Travis rubbed his face. "I want her to be happy, Jessica."

"I never said you did not." She sat down on the bed and looked at him with deep concern in her green eyes. "But this is going to be a big change for her. Even more than being the daughter of a senator."

Travis nodded. The excitement that he had felt earlier was gone. "When will she be home?" he asked again.

"I am not sure," Jessica admitted to him. "for all I know she could be with Michael Kinkade right now."

"Michael Kinkade! We told her to stay away from that punk! She is deliberately disobeying us."

"I have told her to keep away from him. And she said I could not tell her whom she could be friends with. I tried to stop her, but when I got outside she was gone." She got up from the bed and went into the bathroom that was adjutant to the bedroom.

Travis was right behind her. "You did not try hard enough to stop her."

"What would you have had me done, Travis? Call the police?" she opened the medicine cabinet and took out her migraine pills. She popped one in her mouth and swallowed. "You really would have loved to have the police involved."

"You could have done something," he argued. "I can't have Kinkade around to ruin my chances of winning the election."

Jessica slammed the medicine cabinet shut and looked over at Travis. "Who said I wanted you to run?"

"You don't want me to run for president?"

Jessica rubbed her temples as she pushed past Travis. "Let's talk about this when Abby comes home."

Travis pounded the bathroom door in anger. "I am sure she is going to love this conversation as much as you did."

Jessica laid back on the bed and closed her eyes. "I have a feeling you are right."

* * * * * * * * * * *

Six o'clock that night Abby finally returned home. She was not surprised when she saw her parents were waiting on her. Neither one looked too happy. "Well, if it isn't Ozzie and Harriet," she said sarcastically, as she entered the living room.

Travis got up from the couch. "Abby, we need to talk to you." Abby acted like she did not hear him and continued to walk to the stairs. "Abby, get back here now!"

Abby turned around and sat down on the black leather chair that matched the couch. "What do you want?"

Travis stood in front of Abby with his arms folded. "There is something we have to discuss."

"I know what you want to talk about," she glared at her father. "You want me to stop seeing Michael Kinkade. Well, you can't tell what to do."

Travis, who was accustomed to getting respect, was stunned over the lack of respect his own child was giving him. He could remember a time when he and Abby were very close. But all that had changed. "Don't use that tone of voice with me, young lady." He sat down on the couch next to Jessica to show a united front. "We are going to talk right now even if you don't like it."

Abby crossed her legs and showed even more leg. She gave a long sigh. "Okay, what is this about?"

"We are going to talk about Michael first and then we have other matters to discuss," Travis said. He leaned closer to Abby. *I don't even know where to start,* he thought sadly. *How could have let things get so bad between us?* "I told you that you could no longer see that Kinkade boy and you deliberately disobeyed me."

"You can't stop me from seeing Michael. He is the only one that understands me."

11

Jessica took her daughter's hand. "Listen to us, please," she begged. "we only want what is best for you. And Michael is not it. He'll only end up hurting you in the end."

"No, he won't. Michael is the only person that is not hurting me. He loves me for who I am."

"He does not love you, Abby. He is only using you and when he gets what he wants from you he'll dump you," Travis said, touching her shoulder gently.

Abby looked like she was about to cry. Her lower lip trembled and she bit it. She jerked her shoulder away from his touch. "You are the one that is trying to hurt me. You take me away from my friends and then when I make more you don't like them because they are not the 'right' kind of people."

Travis sat back in his chair. He was stunned over the hurt and anger that she was releasing. "Abby, I am in politics. We have to be careful with whom we associate. They could hurt me politically," He explained.

Abby gave a cold smile that sent a chill through her father. "That's all you care about isn't it? Your career." She got up from the chair. "I am done talking."

Travis got up to and grabbed her arm. "We are not done until I say we are done! Now sit down! I have one more thing to say to you."

Abby flopped down on the chair. "You are running for the Senate again, aren't you? Well, I am not surprised. They worship the ground you walk on over there."

Travis swallowed his anger and took a deep breath. "I am thinking about running for president."

Abby looked at him in surprise and then looked over at her mother. "You are going to run for president? Don't I get a say on how I feel about this? Or are you going to ignore my feelings like you usually do?"

"Of course, I care about how you feel, Abby. And I want to know what you think about me running for president."

"Do you really want to know how I feel about this?" Abby asked her father.

Travis nodded his head not really sure he wanted to know how she felt about it. "Yes, I do."

"I hate it," she snapped at him. "I hated it when you ran for the Senate and I would hate being the president's daughter."

"You would get used to it," he said encouragingly.

Abby looked over at Jessica who had not said anything for a few minutes. *Mom probably feels the same as me but Dad doesn't care. He'll do what he wants to do and screw us,* Abby realized. By the look on her mother's face she could tell that she was not happy about it either. "Mom, do you want Dad to run for president?"

"This is not about me, Abby, this is about you," Jessica replied.

Travis looked over at his wife. "I want to know how you feel about it too, Jess."

"I need more time to think about it. This a big decision and it can't be made lightly."

Travis stood up from the couch. "Fine."

"Travis, this is a huge life decision. It can't be made in one night!" she yelled at him as he walked toward the door. She got up from the couch and followed him. "That's right Travis runaway! Just runaway when things don't go your way! That's what you always do!" she screamed at him as he got into his car. He sped off in a cloud of dust. Jessica went back inside and sat back down on the couch and burst into tears.

Abby felt bad for her mother and she got up from the chair and sat down next to her. She put her arms around her and tried to comfort her. "I am sorry." was all she could think of to say.

Jessica put her arms around her to and held her tightly. "I am sorry too, honey," she cried. "I am just worried about you and this family."

Mom knows how we have drifted apart, Abby though sadly, remembering happier times. "What is going to happen to us?" she wondered.

"I don't know. But I worry about you being with Michael Kinkade. I know you think he loves you, but I don't trust him. I want to protect you from all the dangers in the world, but I can't."

"You don't know Michael like I do," she said, as she pulled away from her mother. "He would never hurt me. Unlike some people."

Jessica smoothed Abby's auburn hair. "Your dad doesn't mean to hurt you, Abby. He just wants what's best for you and some times he can come off as unfeeling but he doesn't mean to."

"I wish we were still living in Sunset," Abby admitted. "We were a family when we lived there."

"We are still a family, Abby."

"No, we are not. When we were in Sunset we used to do things together all the time. We would go horseback riding, camping, and weekend trips to Disney World. Now Dad is always busy."

Jessica nodded sadly. She too wished that they were still in Montana. "Things are different now. But, he still loves you."

Abby did not look convinced. "You and Dad are fighting an awful lot."

"I know we are fighting a lot here recently, but we still love one another. And we love you, too. There is nothing that you can do or say that is going to change that." Jessica tried to put her arms around Abby, but she would not let her. "Abby, you have to believe me."

I want to believe you but it's hard, Abby thought. She got up from the couch. "I am going to my room." she said instead. She left her mother sitting in the living room by herself.

* * * * * * * * * * *

The following week Travis came home early. He found his wife and daughter in the family room. Jessica was a reading a murder mystery and Abby was writing in her journal. They both looked up when he came into the room. "I have made my decision," he announced. Abby put her pen down and Jessica shut her book. "I am going to run for president."

Chapter Two

Two days later on a Wednesday, Travis was going to make the public announcement that he would be running for president. Travis stood in front of his bedroom mirror retying his red tie. He looked at Jessica's reflection in the mirror. She pulled a navy skirt and blouse out of her closet. She tossed it on their bed. Instead of acting like she was going to speak to the media, she was acting like she was going to a funeral. He sighed, "You could look happier Jessica. This is a big day for me. Well, for all of us actually."

Jessica put her skirt on and a pair of black pumps. "I know it is an important day for you."

Travis sat down on the bed feeling disappointed. *I wish you could be happy for me,* he thought. He watched her as she continued to get dressed. She had been cold to him for the last couple of days. But much to his great surprise, Abby was actually excited for him. When he had told them he was running for president she actually jumped up from the chair and hugged him. "Abby, is happy for me. Why can't you?"

"I am happy for you, Travis." She never met his eyes. Jessica put on her blouse and then went to the dresser and began putting on her make-up. "I am just nervous about talking to the press this afternoon."

"You have talked to the press before."

"But this time you'll be announcing that you are running for president." She put her shoulder length hair into a low ponytail. She held the ponytail in place with a gold clasp.

"You don't want me to run, do you?"

"Do what makes you happy, Travis." She applied some blush to her face. "I'll get used to this."

Travis stood up and went to the dresser and turned her around so she would look at him. He took her hands in his. "I want you to be happy too, Jessica."

Jessica gave him a weak smile. "I'll be fine and so will Abby. We just need sometime to get used to this." She pulled away from him and finished putting her make-up on.

Travis felt the frustration build in him again. He grabbed his jacket off the chair and put it on. "You need more time," he mumbled. "I am going to go down stairs." He stormed out of their bedroom and into the hall. Just as he got to Abby's room the door opened and he almost ran into her as she came out. "Sorry, honey."

"It's alright, Dad." Abby had on a navy skirt and a white lacey shirt on. She pushed her hair behind her ear. Her green eyes sparkled with excitement. She spun around for him. "What do you think?"

"Beautiful."

"Thanks. Is Mom ready?"

Travis looked toward his bedroom. "She is not excited as you about this as you are. I wish she could be a little more supportive."

"She'll come around." Abby and Travis walked down the stairs.

Travis looked at her and gave her a happy smile. Abby felt a sting a regret. *He deserves this. After all that he has done he deserves this,* she thought, trying to convince herself that she was doing the right thing. "I am happy that you are excited about this. It means a lot to me," he said.

Abby's guilt continued to grow. "I want you to be happy." She smoothed her skirt out and sat down in the recliner.

Travis sat down on the couch next to the chair. "If I asked you a question, would you be honest with me?"

"About what?"

"Why are you beginning so gun-ho about me running for president? You hated it when I ran for the Senate. And now all of a sudden you love the fact that I am running for president. What made you change your mind?" Travis folded his arms and looked at her. He tapped his hand on his arm while he was waiting for her to answer.

Abby looked on the floor and then met her father's eyes. "I just want to be supportive this time."

"Well, I am ready," Jessica said, as she came down the stairs. "Let's get this done and over with."

Travis continued to stare at his daughter. *Something is going on. She is not being honest with me,* he thought. He did not have enough proof that she was up to something. Finally, he got up from his chair and took Jessica's hand. The three of them walked to the door. Travis opened the door and they stepped outside. There were about fifteen to twenty reporters waiting in their front yard. Some of the people had cameras while others had video cameras. "Good afternoon," he called out to them to get their attention.

They hurried over to where the Moores' were standing. The people holding the cameras began snapping pictures. "Senator Moore, are you going to run for president?'

"Are the rumors true?"

"Mrs. Moore, how do you feel about this?"

The questions were asked at one time. Jessica immediately felt overwhelmed, while Travis laughed and held up a hand to get them to quite down. "I am going to make an announcement today." He reached over and pulled Jessica closer to him. He kept his right arm around Jessica and took Abby's hand with his other hand. "My wife and daughter are with me today so they can show their support." He felt Jessica tense up. "I am officially announcing that I am running for President of the United States!"

"Mrs. Moore, how do you feel about your husband running for president?"

"Senator Moore, do you think you have a chance to win?"

"Miss Moore, will you be involved with the election?" The reporters called out their questions to them again.

Travis again raised his hands and they quieted down a little. "We are willing to answer your questions. But one at a time." He gave his family a smile. "To answer your question if I think I can win, the answer is yes. Especially, with my wife and daughter to help me."

The reporters continued shut out their questions, when suddenly the rumble of a motorcycle engine drowned them out. *No. It can't be. She would not do this to me. Not today,* he thought, looking over at Abby.

A motorcycle, a black Harley Davidson, came to a stop behind the reporters and they turned around. They mumbled to one another. The driver pulled his helmet off and shook his greasy black hair free. It was Michael Kinkade. He looked over at Abby and waved. "Are you ready, babe?" he yelled out to Abby.

Travis glared at his daughter. "What is he doing here?"

"Michael!" she cried out happily. She ran across the lawn to him. Abby threw herself into his arms and kissed him deeply. She pulled away from him and hoped on the back of the Harley. "Let's go!" Michael gunned the motor and they sped off.

Jessica felt her heart drop to her stomach. Her eyes filled with tears and she blinked them back. She did not want the cameramen to get a picture of her crying. She looked over at Travis. She could tell that he was seething with anger. "Travis," she said softly.

"Senator, who was that young man?" one reporter asked.

"This press conference is over," he snapped. He pulled Jessica back into the house. He slammed the door shut. "I can't believe that she would do this to me."

Jessica just looked at him. *Yes, you do believe that she would do this. You were just hoping that she wouldn't,* she thought, feeling disappointed in Abby's actions. "I am sorry, Travis."

"I can't believe she would ruin the press the conference."

"You are going to have to talk to her about this," she told him.

Travis opened his briefcase and stuffed some papers inside of it. "I can't believe that she deliberately ruined the press conference. What was she thinking?"

Jessica could not stand the fact that he was going to go to the office, which meant she would have to be the one to talk to their daughter. He always did that. She walked over to the desk and ripped the papers out of his hand and threw them to the floor. "She did it to get your attention, Travis!"

"I don't have time to deal with this. I am going to meet with Brad Johnson to talk about my campaign." He knelt down and picked up the papers. He put them in his briefcase and closed it.

"You should be the one to talk to Abby. She is crying out for your attention."

"You'll have to talk to her, Jessica. I am going to be in meetings all afternoon." He picked up the briefcase and started to walk to the front door.

Jessica was right behind him. He was not going to get off that easy. "We are going to lose our daughter, Travis!" He did not say anything to her. "This is all your fault!" The only answer she got was the slamming of the front door. Jessica picked up a vase that was sitting on the table and flung it at the door.

* * * * * * * * * * * *

Abby finished her beer and tossed her can into the trashcan and reached for another one. "That was great," she told Michael. She popped the can open and took a long swallow. They were at a run down neighborhood park that had been deserted for years. The swings were broken and the slide had graffiti all over it. Basketball nets had been ripped off. The only people that used this park now were the gangs.

Michael drank some of his beer. "I loved the look on old Senator Moore's face when I pulled up," he chuckled.

Abby giggled, too. She reached over and stroked his cheek. "He was pretty mad." She felt even guiltier over what she had done to her parents. Especially, her mother.

21

She shoved her feelings of guilt down. "It served him right, though." She took a big gulp of beer and let out a loud burp. "He doesn't care about how Mom and I really feel. If he did we would still be living in Sunset."

"Then you would have never met me." Michael reached over and pulled her head to him. He gave her a long hard kiss.

Abby closed her eyes and kissed him back. "Meeting you was the only good thing about living here." She finished her second beer and grabbed another beer. She opened it and took a drink.

"Slow down on those, okay?"

"I can handle my booze. So leave me alone."

"This beer as to last me till my next pay day," he told her. "I am going to a couple of guys over tomorrow night and I want them to have something to drink."

Abby was feeling funny, but she did not let on. "Don't worry," she said, slurring her words. "You'll have enough beer. This is going to be my last one."

"I hope so."

Abby fell to the ground spilling some of the beer on her clothes. "I am really worried about my mom," she said suddenly. "She has been really sad these last few days."

Michael did not say anything. He just kept drinking his beer and watching her. He looked bored. He finished his beer and tossed it in the trashcan.

Abby was disappointed that he did not ask if she wanted to talk. He did not really want to know what was going on with her. All he cared about was that she was a fun party girl. *Nobody wants to hear about what is going on with me. They don't want to hear about how I feel. Just once I want someone to honestly care about me,* she thought sadly. She guzzled her beer and finished it up. Abby felt extremely dizzy and her stomach churned. She knew that she was going to be sick to her stomach. She would rather be sick at home than in a run down park. "We should go. My parents are going to have a fit."

"I need to get to going too," Michael said. Abby stood up and then she fell to the ground. "Are you alright?"

Abby nodded. She did not want to tell him how bad she felt. She felt her stomach churn again and she covered her mouth. *I am going to puke,* she thought horrified. She got up on her knees and threw up. She retched a few times, but nothing else came up.

"Are you okay, Abby?" He asked after she finished throwing up. *She does not look good at all,* he thought in a panic. *How will I ever get her home?*

Abby did not answer him. The world was spinning faster and faster. The next thing she knew darkness surrounded her and she passed out.

Chapter Three

Jessica paced the Emergency room lobby. What she wanted to do was run back to the room where they were trying to save Abby's life. *This can't be happening. Any minute I'll wake up and all of this all have been a nightmare,* she thought, for the thousandth time that evening. But she knew that this was no nightmare.

Two people had been walking past the park when they saw Abby passed out. They hurried over to check on her and realized that she needed help. Jessica let a cry as she remembered the call to come to the hospital. *Where's Travis?* she asked. *Why can't he be here when Abby and I need him?* She collapsed into one of the ugly orange plastic chairs and buried her face in her hands.

"Jessica? Jessica, what happened to Abby?"

Jessica looked up when she heard Travis's voice. She got up and hugged him. Not so much to comfort him, but that she needed someone to hold her. "She has alcohol poisoning."

"Alcohol poisoning? How did she get that?"

She pulled away from him. "How do you think?" she snapped. "She was with Michael and they were drinking."

"How is she doing?" he asked ignoring her sarcasm.

She shook her head. "I don't know. They have not told me anything yet." Jessica looked at the nurse manning the Emergency room information desk. "They won't let me go back there."

Travis looked over at the nurse. She gave him a quick glance and then went back to her paper work. "I'll find something out." He walked over to the desk and banged on the desk with a fist. She looked up at him annoyed, but he did not care. "I want to know how my daughter, Abby Moore, is doing."

"Take a seat and the doctor will be out to talk to you as soon as he can," she told him and went back to her work.

He wanted to yank the paper out of her hand, but could not get to her thanks to the protective barer between them. "Listen," he snapped. "I want to know what is going on with my daughter, and I want to know now."

She sighed, "Senator, I know that you are upset, but you'll have to wait till the doctor comes out. Now please sit down or I'll call security."

Jessica walked up to him and took his arm. "Travis, please just sit down. This is not going to help Abby."

Travis let his wife take him back to the plastic orange chairs and he sat down. He rubbed his forehead with a shaky hand. "This is Kinkade's fault. If I ever see that boy again, I'll kill him."

"He did not force Abby to drink. She made the decision on her own. And talk like that won't help her," his wife said, touching his arm gently.

"I know." *To tell the truth this is my fault. If I had been a better father she would never have ran off with that boy. She would not be in there fighting for her life,* thought Travis.

The door to the Emergency room opened and the desk nurse called them back. They went in and went up to the nurse who was standing next to a young man in green scrubs and a lab coat. He slouched a little like he was exhausted. "Senator and Mrs. Moore, this is Doctor Martin. He has been treating your daughter."

Travis shook hands with the young man, Jessica asked, "How is my daughter?"

Dr. Martin rubbed his eyes with his fingers. "It was touch and go there for awhile," he admitted to them. "There was a lot of alcohol in her system. But she is stable now. I'll take you back to see her." He led them to a cubicle and pushed back the curtain. "We are going to send her to a room in a few minutes."

Jessica went in first and hurried to the bed. She sucked in a breath when she saw Abby. Abby's face was pale as snow. There were I.V. lines attached to her arms and an oxygen tube in her nose. She took her daughter limp hand in hers and squeezed it. "Oh, baby."

"She'll be conscious by tomorrow," Dr. Martin said, trying to give them some comfort. He looked from Jessica to Travis with concern in his brown eyes. "There is someone I want you to meet. She'll meet us in Abby's room."

"Who is it?" Travis asked his eyes on his daughter.

"She is a councilor," he held up a hand to keep Travis from interrupting him. "When a sixteen year old girl nearly kills herself with alcohol, there is something serious going on."

Jessica looked at her husband. "We need someone to help us with Abby. She needs help." She touched her daughter's forehead. "I don't want my daughter to die. I can't lose her."

Travis walked over to the bed and took Abby's hand. She looked dead to him and his heart stopped. He leaned over and whispered in her ear, "I am here, baby. It's Daddy." He squeezed his eyes shut and a couple of tears came out. "I love you."

Jessica watched her husband. She looked back down at her unconscious daughter. She wanted to say something comforting to Travis, but nothing came to mind. In fact if she was truly honest to herself, she was mad at him. She blamed him for this.

Two orderlies came into the cubicle. "Dr. Martin, the room is ready for her."

Dr. Martin nodded and turned to the Moore's. "Let's get her to the room." He indicated for them to go out into the hall. "When we get her to the room, I'll introduce you two to Melissa Connor."

Travis and Jessica stepped out into the hall. "I don't think Abby needs to see this councilor. She is just experimenting with alcohol. A lot of kids her age experiment. Now that she has seen what can happen to her. She won't drink again," Travis told her.

"You really believe that?"

"Yes."

Jessica glared at him. "I know why you believe that, Travis. Your political career is more important to you," she said. "You would rather be president than help our daughter."

Travis did not say anything. *You don't understand. You don't know what it is like to have someone you love die because of alcohol.* He opened his mouth to defend himself, but could not bring himself to tell her. "That's not true. I want what is best for Abby. I would do anything for her."

"Then let's talk to this counselor. She knows the best way to give Abby the help she needs! Who cares what everyone thinks! What is important is that we help Abby the best we can." Jessica put a hand on his arm.

Travis looked into Jessica's pleading green eyes. He sighed, "Okay, we'll talk to this Connor woman."

* * * * * * * * * * * *

The next morning Abby was sitting up in bed eating breakfast when her parents came into her hospital room. "Hi," she said in a horse voice.

Jessica sat down in the chair next to the bed. She reached over and smoothed her hair out of her face. "How are you feeling this morning?"

"Better."

"I am glad," Jessica admitted. She looked over at Travis and he nodded at her. "Last night your father and I spoke to a councilor."

Abby looked from her mother to her father. "You did?" she asked suspiously.

"Yes, we did. Her name is Melissa Connor and we liked her. She is going to be in later this afternoon to speak to you," Jessica told her.

"I don't need a shrink."

"Abby, you are an alcoholic. You need help. I don't want to be called to identify your body in the morgue."

Abby looked over at Travis. He had not said a single word since arriving at the hospital. "Dad, don't force me to see a shrink. I have learned my lesson. I won't drink again."

Travis stepped into the room. "Abby, you nearly killed yourself last night."

"Dad, I know I messed up yesterday, but I learned my lesson. I won't do this again. I won't see Michael anymore. Please, don't make me see a shrink or let them lock me up somewhere."

Travis walked over to Jessica and took her arm. *Maybe it would be best if Jessica handled Abby's problems ourselves,* he thought. *No need for outside forces to interfere. Hopefully, we can keep this incident quite.* "I want to talk to you out in the hall for a minute."

Jessica gave him a confused look. "Okay," she said reluctantly. She gave Abby a reassuring smile. "We'll be right back, honey." She followed him out to the hall and dropped her smile. "What is this about, Travis? We agreed at home that she needs professional help."

"I know what we agreed on, Jessica. But you need to think about the big picture. If the press gets a hold of this they'll be hounding her."

"And it will paint you in a bad light, won't it? The perfect image that you want to pass of would be seen as a lie. And you can't have that can you, Travis?"

"I was just thing about what's best for us."

"No," she said in disappointment. "you are thinking about what is best for you. I am going to take her to see Miss Connor." Jessica turned and went back into her daughter's room.

"Were you two talking about me?"

"Yes, we were talking about the best way to help you." Jessica looked at Travis as if she were daring him to say otherwise. "We both agree that you need to have treatment for your alcoholism."

"I am not a alcoholic!" snapped Abby. "I drink to help me relax. Living with the two of you I need to find some way to relax."

29

Travis felt a sharp pain in the heart. *She is so unhappy and angry. How can I help her get through this?* He asked himself. He wanted to give her a hug, but he could not bring himself to do it. He thought back to last night. Fear gripped him. *She could have ended up like...no I am not going to think like that.* "I am sorry, but I have to go," he said suddenly. He had to get out of the hospital or he would go crazy.

Jessica was alarmed by the expression on his face. "Travis, what's wrong? Are you sick?"

"No, I just remembered an important meeting I have in twenty minutes," he lied. "Do want me to take a cab? That way you'll still have my car."

"I can take a cab." *What's going on with him?* Jessica asked herself. *He looks absolutely sick.* He nodded at her and hurried out of the room. She turned her attention back to Abby. "You really shook your father up. He was up half the night pacing the floor because of you." She left out the part that they had a huge fight, and Travis ended up sleeping in the guest bedroom.

"Probably worried that I am ruining his chances of winning the presidency." Abby blinked back tears.

"That's not true, Abby," argued Jessica. "That's not true at all. He was very upset about you last night. We talked about what was the best way to help you."

Abby looked out the window. "I just want to go home." She looked up at her mother with pleading eyes. "Please, Mom, can I go home? I'll feel better in my own room, in my own bed. I'll do whatever you want me to. I'll talk to this councilor. I'll go to A.A meetings. Just tell me what you want me to do and I'll do it." She could see that she was making headway with her mother. "It'll make Dad happier to have me home," she added.

Jessica was not totally convinced that it was a good idea. She sat down on the bed and looked into Abby's eyes. "I want you to promise me that you will talk to Miss Connor. And that you will go to A.A meetings. I want your word that you won't drink any more."

Abby realized that this was a test in trust. If she broke her promise it could destroy their relationship. She felt a sting of doubt about leaving. The feeling was gone as fast as it came. She would do anything to get out of the hospital. She met her mother's stare, "I promise, Mom. I won't let you down."

Jessica sighed and stood up. "I am trusting you, Abby. I hope I am not making a mistake." She headed toward the door. "I'll look for Dr. Martin so we can get you out of here."

Abby was extremely happy with herself. She got what she had wanted. She was going to get out of this hellhole. Ten minutes later her mother and Dr. Martin came into her room. "Hi, Doc."

Dr. Martin gave her a wary smile and sat down in the chair next to the bed. "Hi, Abby. Your mother tells me you want to check out of the hospital."

"Yes, I want to go home. I'll do better at home than here," she told him. "I told my mother that I'd talk to Miss. Connor and do A.A meetings."

"There is no medical reason for me to keep you here," Dr. Martin said. He did not look that happy about it. "I don't think you understand that you almost died last night."

"I drank too much last night. I won't do it again."

Dr. Martin leaned closer to Abby. "You are an alcoholic and you are in denial about it." He looked over at Jessica, "You and your husband are in denial over this, too."

Jessica sighed in frustration. "I know that my daughter has problems. And I am going to do my best to help her. As for my husband, he is a busy man. But he'll do what he needs to do to help Abby."

Dr. Martin did not look convinced. "I know that you think you are doing what is best for Abby, but the truth you could be doing more harm than good. I think she should stay here until we can get her into a treatment center."

Jessica was alarmed. She could tell by Abby's expression she was upset as well. *I am glad Travis is not here. He would be having a fit right now. He would have dragged Abby out of the hospital the minute Dr. Martin mentioned the treatment center,* she thought to herself. She bit her lip. "I think the best thing would be to take Abby home. I don't think she needs to go to a treatment center."

"I can't force you to admit Abby to the treatment center. But I will give you information on the center here at the hospital. Maybe, you'll change your mind." Dr. Martin got up.

"Okay."

"I'll get your paper work started so you can go home," he said, as he left the room.

Jessica sat down in the chair that Dr. Martin had been sitting in and rubbed her forehead. "I hope I did the right thing."

Abby gave her a reassuring smile. "You did, Mom. I promise I won't drink again."

* * * * * * * * * * *

When Travis came home later that night he was surprised to find Abby in the living room. "Abby! You're home! I am glad." He sat his brief case on the coffee table and leaned over and gave her a hug.

Abby shrugged him off. "I am sure you are happy that I am home. That way you don't have to worry about the press finding out I was in the hospital for alcohol poisoning." She got off the couch and stormed upstairs.

I can't do anything right with her, he thought sadly. *Maybe, I'll do better with her mother.* He went into their sunny kitchen. Jessica was sitting at the table drinking tea. She looked at him and gave him a weak smile. Travis walked over to her and bent down to give her a kiss on the top of her head. "Hi, honey."

"Hi, Travis," she said in a tired voice.

Travis sat down across from her. "I am glad Abby was able to come home. What did Dr. Martin say to you?"

Jessica took a sip of her tea and sat the cup down. "He thinks Abby needs to be admitted to the treatment center for drug abuse. He gave me some information about one." She got up and poured more hot water into her tea. She looked at him over her shoulder and asked, "Do you want any tea?"

"No, thanks. I am fine." He slouched in his chair. *A treatment center? Is Abby really an alcoholic?* Travis wondered. "What do you think?"

Jessica met his blue eyes. She could see the fear in them and it tugged at her heart. "I do believe that she is an alcoholic. I think we should see how she does with A.A meetings. She promised me she would go and talk to Miss. Connor."

"A.A meetings? I don't know if that is a good idea. What if someone saw her at one of those meetings."

"So what if they did see her? She'll be getting help for her problem." It suddenly dawned on her what he was concerned with. "I understand what your problem is, Travis. You are worried that someone from the media will see her."

Travis pounded his fist on the table. He was worried about that, but not for the reasons she thought. "Yes, I'm worried that the press will get a hold of this. I can just see the headlines now. 'Presidential Candidate's daughter is an alcoholic'. How do you think Abby will feel if she sees those headlines?"

"I don't care about the press, Travis, I care about our daughter!" She yelled at him. "Our daughter needs us more now than she ever has before! We have to help her get through this."

"I am going to help her. I will support her." *But it won't be good enough for you. I have been through this before and I could not save him,* Travis thought helplessly. He did not say anything to her. He walked over to the window. He leaned against the wall and looked out. "I don't know what to do to help her. She won't talk to me, Jessica. When I came in I told her I was glad she was home and all she did was get up and leave."

Jessica got up and went to him. She put her arms around him and hugged his back. She did not say anything. There was not much she could say to him that would make him feel better. They stayed like that for several minutes, eventually Jessica let him go. He did not turn from the window. Travis looked so sad that it broke her heart. *There is more going on with him than he is telling me,* she thought, *I wish he would open up and tell me what is going on. I could help him.* "Travis?"

"Hmm?"

She made him turn around and forced him to look at him. "Travis, there is something else bothering you isn't there?" Travis did not answer her. Instead he walked past her. "How can you help Abby if you won't let anyone help you?" Jessica demanded.

Chapter Four

Jessica woke up with a start. She heard a noise, but she was not sure what it was. She heard the sound again. She looked over to see if Travis had heard the noise, but he was not in bed. *Where is he?* Jessica wondered. She noticed that the bathroom light was on. Jessica rolled over and got out of bed. The bathroom door was ajar and the she could hear him in there. She pushed the door open and went in. Travis was sitting on the floor in the corner crying. His hands were covered his face and his body shook with sobs. She hurried to his side, "Travis? What's wrong?" She touched him gently on the shoulder.

Travis wiped his eyes with the back of his hands and took in a deep breath. "I am sorry, I did not mean to wake you up."

She knelt beside him and rubbed his back. "It's okay. I understand. I am worried about Abby too."

He laid his head back against the wall and looked at the ceiling. "I had a nightmare," he admitted. "but I can't remember what the dream was about. All I know is it scared the hell out of me."

Jessica continued to rub his back. "It's over now, Travis."

"It doesn't feel like it is over," he whispered.

Jessica gave him a hug and stood up. "Come on, honey, let's get off this cold floor." She helped Travis stand up. "Let's go back to bed." She took his arm and pulled him out of the bathroom. Jessica was stunned to see that he was trembling. *He is sure shaken up over this nightmare,* she thought watching him.

"I am cold," he said through chattering teeth. "I am so cold." Jessica pulled back the bed sheets and put Travis in bed. "You are not going to leave me? Are you?"

His vulnerability tugged at her heart. She gave him a motherly smile and smoothed his hair out of his face. "Of course not. I am going to be right here." She got into bed on her side and scooted over so she could put her arms around him. "Is that better?"

Travis held her tightly. "Don't let me go. Please, Jessica, whatever you do, don't let me go," he begged. Jessica tightened her hold on him. She did not say anything to him. She stroked his thick hair. Travis felt the tears fall down his cheeks. He buried his head in her shoulder.

Jessica felt her own tears run down her cheeks. Neither of them said a word and neither went back to sleep.

* * * * * * * * * * *

"Mom, you don't have to hover over me," Abby said to Jessica the following morning. "I am fine."

Jessica stepped into the messy room. She maneuvered through clothes, magazines, and books that cluttered the floor. She sat down on the unmade bed. She gave Abby a strained smile. "I am not hovering, Abby. I was just checking to see how you slept last night. And if you needed anything."

37

Abby got up from her desk and walked over to the bed. She shoved some clothes off of it and sat down next to her mother. She got a better look of her mother's tired face. She felt her heart constrict. "You look tired."

"Your father and I did not sleep very well last night," Jessica admitted with a yawn.

"Why don't you take a nap. I'll be fine." Abby pointed over to the desk where her math book was lying open. "I have homework I need to make up." Abby was determined to be a better person. She thought that if she stayed busy she would stay out of trouble.

Jessica let out another yawn that cracked the side of her lips. *Ouch,* she thought touching them. "I think I will try to take a nap." She got off the bed and walked to the door. She looked over her shoulder, "Promise me that you won't leave the house. You need your rest too."

"I'll stay right here."

"Good." She left Abby's room and went down the hall to her bedroom. She rubbed her tired eyes, *Maybe, I'll feel better after a nap,* Jessica thought. She went into her room and saw Travis sitting on the bed. He had his black suite pants and a white dress shirt on. She thought he planned on staying home.

He looked up when he heard her. "How's Abby?"

"Why don't you ask her yourself?"

Travis picked up his tie and went to the mirror. He put it around his neck and tied it. "I tried to get her to talk to me, but she won't."

Jessica gave a frustrated sigh. *I have heard this story over and over again. I am sick of hearing it. Why can't he just try harder?* She asked herself. "Keep working at it. You can't give up."

"I don't know what else to do." He met her gaze in the reflection of the mirror.

Jessica decided to change the subject. "Travis, about last night..."

He turned from the mirror and grabbed his shoes that were by the wall. "I don't want to talk about last night," he interrupted. Travis sat down on the bed to put his shoes on.

Fine shut me out, she thought angrily. She changed the subject again. "Melissa Connor is coming this afternoon. I think we both should be here."

Travis shook his head. "There is a Senate hearing today over the tobacco issue. I have to be there. And right after that, I am meeting with Senator Johnson to discuss my campaign."

"Can't you postpone your meeting with Brad until tomorrow?" Jessica asked.

"I am sorry, Jessica. It's just not possible." He got up from the bed and slipped on his jacket. "He is leaving tomorrow for Ohio to campaign for his own re-election."

Jessica felt her frustration, anger, and hurt grow. "Then meet with him when he gets back. Today is Abby's first counseling session and I wanted her to see that we both support her in her recovery process."

"I do support her. But I don't think she really needs to see this councilor. This was a one time occurrence and I don't think it will happen again," Travis argued. He picked up his briefcase from the table. He began to fill it with the papers and other things that he would need for the day.

Jessica wanted to grab the briefcase away from him, but she knew that it would not do her any good. *He is in denial over Abby. I wish he would open his eyes and see that she is in trouble. Instead he always runs away when we need him most,* Jessica thought. "You don't want to face the truth! The truth could destroy you, couldn't it?" She folded her arms and glared at him. "What's more important to you, Travis? Us or your career?"

Travis met her gaze with an angry one of his own. He slammed his briefcase shut in an angry thud. "You and Abby are the most important people in my life! I would do anything for the two of you!" *How many times do I have to tell you that? Why can't you believe me?* Travis asked silently.

"I wish I could believe that."

Travis opened the door to the bedroom and stepped out into the hall. "I wish you could believe me too, Jessica."

After he left, Jessica began to cry. She threw herself on the bed and buried her face into a pillow. The stress of arguing with Travis and worrying about Abby came pouring out of her. She did not even hear someone come into her room until she felt a hand on her shoulder. She rolled over and saw Abby standing next to the bed. "Mom, what's going on? I heard you and Dad yelling at each other."

"It's nothing for you to worry about."

Abby reached over to the nightstand and pulled out some tissues and handed them to her mother. "You were arguing over me. Weren't you?"

"Partly," Jessica admitted, as she wiped her eyes and blew her nose. "But there are other things going on as well. I don't like the fact that he is putting his career before us. And he is using work to hide from his problems."

Abby nodded. She had heard that part of their argument. *He is working more so he doesn't have to deal with me,* Abby realized. She felt herself tense up. *I want a drink. No, I don't. It will just add more problems,* she argued with herself.

Jessica got up from the bed and walked to the huge window. She looked out to the garden in the backyard. "I hate this."

Abby did not know what to say. She was being eaten alive by her own guilt. She had to get out of the bedroom before her mother's grief and her own guilt overwhelmed her. "I'll leave you alone." She turned and hurried out of the room. She headed downstairs to her father's study. *I can't handle all this drama. Don't they care what their arguing is doing to me?* Abby thought, feeling her frustration at her parents grow.

Abby walked into her father's immaculate study. Everything was in its place. His desk was not like hers. Everything was neat and tidy. The room smelled of her father. She almost expected him to pop up from behind the desk. She went to an oak cabinet that was in the corner. She knew that her father kept his alcohol in there. She pulled at the two little doors and they would not budge. "Damn it!"

Abby checked the top of the cabinet. The key was not up there. She felt underneath the cabinet to see if it had fallen down there. Again she did not find it. She had the urge to tear the room apart until she found the key. Abby went to his desk and found the key to the cabinet sitting on Travis's leather planner. She felt relief shoot through her. She grabbed it and went back to the cabinet. She stuck the key into the keyhole and unlocked it. The cabinet popped right open reveling the bottles of booze that Travis had on hand to serve his guests. Abby pulled out a bottled of scotch. It was one of her favorites. She opened the bottle and took a long swallow. "Ah, that hit the spot."

"Abigail Lynn Moore!"

Abby turned around slowly. She still had the bottle of scotch in her hand. *Busted,* she thought.

Jessica stormed into the study and yanked the bottle out of her hand. "How could you, Abby?" She took the scotch bottle and dumped it in a plotted plant that was by the door. She locked the cabinet and put the key in her pants pocket. Jessica went to Travis's desk and flipped through his address book. "I am going to call Melissa." She picked up the receiver and dialed the number.

＊＊＊＊＊＊＊＊＊＊＊

Travis came home as soon as he could. Jessica was in the living room waiting for him. "How is Abby?" he demanded.

"I caught her drinking your scotch," she told him. He tried giving her a hug, but she moved out of the way. "How could keep that stuff in this house after she nearly drank herself to death."

Travis collapsed on to a chair. He felt like the wind had been knocked out of him. "I know I should have thrown that stuff out the minute she came home."

"Why didn't you?"

Travis shook his head and stared off into space. "I did not want to believe she has a drinking problem. I just thought that Dr. Martin was being over zealous. I thought he was trying to look like a big shot in front of us and his colleagues."

Jessica sat down next to him. "Now do you believe that Abby has a drinking problem? We have to protect her from all temptations."

Travis got up and headed toward his study. "I better get rid of the alcohol that I have."

"I already did that."

He was grateful that she had gotten rid of the alcohol. Travis was not much of a drinker. He hadn't been since that night. "So where is Abby?"

"Melissa Connor took her to an A.A. meeting. She is going to be Abby's sponsor."

Travis sat back down in the chair and took Jessica's hand. "I am sorry about this morning. It's just that..." he drifted off, "well, it's just everything."

Jessica squeezed his hand to show that she understood what he was trying to tell her. "I am sorry too, Travis. I hate it when we argue."

Travis gave her a loving smile and leaned closer to her. "Yeah, but you want to know the great thing about fighting?" he whispered. He stroked her hair with a hand.

Jessica giggled. "What's that?" she whispered back.

He kissed her sweetly and said, "The making up part."

"So that is what you are up to."

"Is it working?"

Jessica pulled away from him. She could not remember the last time they made love. It seemed like they were always fighting. And she was tired of it. "It could be." She kissed him again, this time it was more passionate.

Travis gently pushed her back against the couch. "I love you, Jessie."

"Love you too, Travis."

They made love on the couch in the living room. After they finished they held each other. Travis kissed her forehead and tightened his grip on her. "That was great."

"Yes, it was," Jessica agreed. She knew that making love would not solve their problems, but it sure beat arguing with him. She cuddled up to him in his arms. "We should do that more often." She kissed him and they made love again. This time when they finished they put their clothes back on.

"Where is the A.A meeting held at?" Travis asked as he put his shirt on and buttoned it.

Jessica pulled her top on and straightened it. "I think that Melissa said it was at the First Assembly of God Church." She checked her watch. "They should be home in about twenty minutes."

Travis tucked his shirt into his pants. "I hope that no one finds out," he muttered under his breath.

Jessica looked over at him with narrowed eyes. "What did you say?" She hoped that she had not heard what she thought she heard.

"Nothing."

She stood in front of him. "I thought you said something like you hoped no one would see them. Was that what you said?" *There for a minute I thought he was going to be supportive of Abby,* Jessica thought seething.

Travis sighed, "Yes, that's what I said. I just don't want someone from the media to see her coming out of an A.A meeting. The press would have a field day."

"I can't believe you said that!" she yelled at him.

Jessica shook her head and stormed upstairs to her room. Travis was right behind her. "What's wrong? I thought you wanted Abby protected." He was confused over her behavior. One minute they were making love the next she was cold toward him.

"I do want Abby protected. But I wonder about you, Travis. I wonder what you really want to protect. Your career or Abby."

Travis grabbed her by the arm and yanked her round so that she would be forced to look at him. "I love my daughter, Jessica. I will do anything I have to do to protect her. And I am tired of you accusing me of not doing enough to do so." Jessica tried to pull away, but Travis put both his hands on her shoulders, "I love my career and I love my family. I have no plans to give either of them up."

Jessica's eyes filled with tears, "I never asked you to give up your career, Travis. I just don't want you to sacrifice Abby or me for your career."

Travis dropped his hands and stared at the floor. He opened his mouth and closed it several times. "I am not going to," he said weakly. *Why is she doing this to me?* he asked himself.

"You say that you won't. But, I don't know." She met his dark blue eyes with hers. "What if the press were to find out about Abby's problems? Would you defend her to the media? Would you stand behind her?"

Travis turned his head and looked out the window. He could not truly answer her. He hated himself for it.

Jessica felt like she had the wind knocked out of her. She sat down on the bed and covered her face with her hands. *How could we go from making love to...to this?* Jessica felt her heart break in half. "If you can't defend Abby to everyone, then I can't be with you."

Travis sat down on the bed next to her. "Don't say that," he begged. He tried to touch her, but she jerked away from him. "Don't do this."

After a few minutes Jessica dropped her hands and looked at him dully. She could not believe that things were falling apart so quickly. But then again things had not been right between them for a long time. She had to be strong. "We need time apart."

"Why are you doing this? We just made love. I thought things were going to be better between us. Why are you

45

doing this to me? To us?" a very hurt and confused Travis asked.

"Because, I am not sure that you would do everything in your power to protect this family," she said. "You have not convinced me that Abby and I are your top propriety." She looked at him with suspicion in her eyes. "And I get the feeling that you are keeping something from me." Jessica got up and went to the closet and pulled out a suitcase.

"I don't want a separation, Jessica. Tell me how I can fix this."

"You can't just fix what is wrong with us." She opened the suitcase. She was amazed that she was so calm.

Travis realized that Jessica's mind was made up and there was nothing he could do to change it. He got up and went to her. He took the suitcase from her. "I'll move out. It'll be easier if I move." He went to the closet and took the clothes that he wanted and threw them on the bed. He began to pack them. Travis looked over at Jessica, who was watching him.

Jessica could feel the tears starting to come. She wanted to throw herself in his arms and tell him that she did not want him to go. But she could not. Until he came to terms with Abby's problems that they could not be together. And until he confided in her what else was bothering they may never be a family again.

Travis finished packing his suitcase and picked up. He headed toward the door. He stopped in front of Jessica. With his free hand he tipped her head up to look at him. Tears had soaked her face and there were more running down her face. He kissed her gently. "I love you." He left the room and walked down the stairs.

Just as he was opening the front door Abby was about to put her key in the lock. "Dad! Where are you going?"

she asked when she saw his suitcase. She felt concerned when she saw that her father was upset. "What's going on?"

Travis took her arm and pulled her into the house. He did not want the neighbors to overhear their conversation. "Your mother and I just need sometime apart to think about what we want out of our relationship," he explained to her.

"Are you going to get divorced?" she asked in a small voice. Tears filled her green eyes. *I don't want my family to split up,* she thought.

The one thing Travis could not stand was when his little girl was upset. "No, we are not going to get a divorce. We just need sometime apart. Don't worry sweetie, before you know it we'll be a family again!"

"Dad, you don't have to talk to me like I am five. I know that you and Mom have been having problems. And a lot if them are caused by me."

Travis sat the suitcase down and forced her to meet his gaze. "Hey, this is not your fault. If it's anyone's fault its mine." He hugged her. "Would you do me a favor?"

Abby pulled away. "What?" She wiped the tears off of her face.

"Take care of your mother for me."

"I will."

Travis gave her another bear hug. "This won't be forever, okay?"

Abby did not say anything to him.

* * * * * * * * * * *

Sometime during the night, Jessica left her bed and went downstairs to the family room. She fell asleep on the couch and that is where Abby found her the next morning.

"Mom? Mom, it's time to wake up." She gave her mother's shoulder a gentle shake.

Jessica opened her eyes and was greeted by the sunlight pouring into the room through the picture window. She covered her face and moaned. She did not feel like she had gotten much sleep. "I am awake." She struggled to sit up. Jessica suddenly remembered what had transpired the night before.

"Did you sleep down here all night?"

"Most of the night," she admitted. "After twenty years of marriage it was hard sleeping by myself."

Abby sat down on the floor next to the couch. She was still in the black stretch shorts and white t-shirt that she slept in. "Dad was pretty upset last night too. I wonder how he did last night."

Jessica ruffled Abby's hair and gave a wistful smile. "When he calls, why don't you talk to him? I know he would love to talk to you."

Abby shrugged her thin shoulders. To tell the truth she was not sure she wanted to talk to him. She was pretty mad at both of them. She did not understand why they could not work things out. The phone rang and Jessica reached to the small table next to the couch where the phone was and picked it up. "Hello, Moore residence."

"Hi, Jess," Travis said. " I wanted to check on you and Abby."

Jessica swallowed hard and blinked back a few tears. "I am fine. Abby and I were just talking about you. We were wondering how you were."

"I miss you both," he confessed. "I just wanted you to know I am at the Rosemont Hotel. The room number is 125. And the phone number is 812-6745."

Jessica wrote down the information on a small note pad. "Thanks." She paused and looked at Abby. *Please, talk to him.* she mouthed to her. Abby nodded. "Travis, Abby would like to speak to you for a minute."

She handed the phone to Abby. "Hi, Dad."

"Hi, honey. I miss you already."

"I am sure."

Travis did not say anything. He knew that she blamed him for their family's problems. "We'll be together soon."

"Dad, do me a favor and don't make any promises that you can't keep." She handed the phone back to Jessica and stormed out of the room.

Jessica watched her daughter with concern. "What did you say to her, Travis? She is upset."

"I told her that this separation wouldn't last long. That we will be a family again soon. I wanted to sound optimistic."

"Travis, you shouldn't have said that to her. No wonder she is so upset. I have to go."

Travis sighed sadly, "I know you want to check on Abby. Tell her I love her. I call again soon."

"Bye, Travis."

"Bye." He hung the phone up. *That did not go the way I had hoped,* he thought.

Jessica hung her phone up and kept a hand on it for a few seconds as if she were touching his hand. *That did not go the way I had hoped,* Jessica thought as well. She stood up and went to Abby's room.

Abby was blasting Alanis Morissette's song, *Uninvited,* at full volume. Jessica banged on the door and yelled her name. When Abby did not answer her she did it again. Frustrated, Jessica opened the door and went in. Abby was lying on her unmade bed. She was not paying any attention to her. Jessica walked to the foot of the bed. "Abby!" she screamed at the top of her lungs.

Abby finally looked over at her mother. "Mom, I thought we agreed that you were going to knock before coming in!" she yelled over the music.

"I knocked twice and you never heard me. And I am not surprised with how loud that music playing."

Abby got up from the bed and turned the stereo off. "What do you want?"

"I know that you are mad at daddy but..."

"I am mad at you, too," Abby interrupted.

Jessica felt her heart break. She knew that had been coming, but it still hurt. She could not deal with Abby right now. "You need to get ready for school. We'll talk more when you get home." She headed out of the room.

"Mom?"

"Yes, Abby?"

Abby sat down on the bed and looked at her mother. "Do you still love Dad?"

Jessica went back to the bed and sat down. "Yes, I love your father very much."

"Then why did he throw him out?"

She knew that she would have to answer that question sooner or later. Jessica had been hoping for later. "It's complicated."

"Complicated," Abby repeated.

She pulled Abby into a hug and gave her a kiss on her forehead. "You just have to believe me when I tell you that the reason why I asked your father to leave was so that you would be protected."

Abby pulled away from her mother. *She is lying. They split so his political career would be protected. Dad can't let it get out that I nearly drank myself to death. He has to distance himself from me,* she thought, her anger at them growing. *They are more concerned about his career than me.* Abby started getting her clothes together for school. "I better get ready."

Jessica got up and walked out into the hall. *I did not help her all. She is still upset. Travis and I are going to have sit down with her and convince her that this is not her fault,* she thought. A half an hour later the phone rang. Jessica picked up the hall extension thinking it would be Travis. "Hello?"

"Hello. Is this the Moore residence?" a male voice asked.

It was not Travis. She did not recognize the voice. He sounded younger than Travis. She thought maybe he was a new friend of Abby's. "Yes, it is. May I help you?"

"Mrs. Moore, this is James Wilson. I am a reporter from, 'The Voice.' We have heard that Senator Moore has moved out. Do you have a comment?"

Chapter Five

Travis walked across the parking lot of his office building. "Senator Moore!" He heard someone call out to him. Travis turned and saw a young man hurrying across the parking lot towards him. "May I speak with you for a moment?"

Travis met the young man half way. He looked vaguely familiar to him. He had seen somewhere but he was not sure where. *He must be a senate page,* he thought, as he approached him. "Yes?" he asked still trying to place him.

He flashed Travis a sparkling smile and held out a hand to Travis. "I am James Wilson from the, 'The Voice.' I would like to ask you about your separation from your wife. Were you having an affair? Or was your wife cheating on you?" He pulled out a small recorder out of his pocket and held it out to Travis. "Do you have a comment?"

Travis grabbed the recorder from him and threw it on the ground. "I have no comment." He pushed past the reporter. He opened the door to the building he looked at James over his shoulder. "Besides, I would never give a comment to, 'The Voice.' All that paper does is print lies. If your editor prints one word about me or my family, I'll sue."

"Can I quote you?"

Travis ignored the reporter and went inside. He took the elevator to the third floor where his office was. He went into his office and told Amy good morning.

"Good morning, sir. Senator Johnson is waiting for you in your office. He is not in a good mood."

"He is not the only one," Travis muttered under his breath and went into his office. Senator Johnson was sitting at Travis's mahogany desk. His feet were propped up on the desk. "Make yourself at home, Brad. Can I get you anything?" he asked sarcastically.

Brad stood up. "Don't start with me, Travis. This has not been a good morning. Guess who called me this morning?"

"Could it have been a reporter from the well-respected newspaper, 'The Voice?' And could the reporter have been James Wilson?"

Brad looked surprised His eyes narrowed slightly. "How did you know?"

"I ran into him in the parking lot." He indicated for Brad to move out of the way so he could sit down in his chair. "He knew about Jessica and me separating."

Brad rubbed his forehead with a hand as if he were getting a headache. "You did not say anything to the press did you?"

"No."

He sat down in a chair in front of the desk. He spoke in low tones as if he were afraid that there were listening devises in the office. "Could Jessica have said anything?"

Travis was offended that he would even suggest something like that. "Of course not! She knows how much that would upset Abby."

Brad did not look convinced. "She might have said something anyway to get revenge on you."

"Jessica would never do that." He could see that Brad was thinking about accusing Abby, but he was going to put a stop to that. "And neither would Abby. They might be mad at me right now. But they would not do something like that to me."

Brad leaned back in his leather chair. "Okay, if you are sure. What about Amy? Is she loyal to you? Would she do something like this?"

"She is very loyal. She wouldn't betray me. I can't think of anyone who could have told, 'The Voice.'"

Brad sighed in frustration, "You are not helping me at all." He got up and began to pace around the spacious room. "Nobody wants to hurt you. No one wants to see you destroyed."

Travis was getting a serious headache. He opened the top drawer to his desk and pulled out an sprain bottle. "Maybe, it someone from O'Neil's campaign. They could have found out some how."

"We are going have to do some damage control." Brad headed toward the door. "I'll think of something that might undo the damage. I'll be in touch."

"I am going to check on Jessica."

"Good," Brad said and was gone.

Travis waited till Abby was home from school before he went to the house. From the office to the house was about a fifteen-minute drive. Today it seemed like it took longer to get there. He got caught in a traffic jam and hit every stoplight. Soon he was pulling into the circular drive. He turned off the motor and headed up to the house. *My own house and now I have to ring the bell,* he thought, ringing the doorbell. Jessica opened the door. "Hi, Jessica."

"Travis, what are you doing here?" she asked in surprise.

"I need to speak with you," he pointed inside the house. "Can I come in?"

Jessica stepped aside quickly. "Oh yeah, sorry," she stammered. She knew why he was there. And it was not to see her and Abby. Travis stepped into the house and followed her into the living room. Jessica stood at the foot of the stairs and called upstairs, "Abby, your father's here!"

Abby grudgingly came down the stairs. "What do you want?"

Travis gave her a smile and walked over to her. He gave her a hug. She felt stiff in his arms and she did not hug him back. He felt his heart break. He watched her as she flopped down on the couch. Jessica looked between Abby and Travis with a sad expression. "Don't talk to your father like that."

"Sorry," she said, not sounding the least bit sorry.

Travis felt his shoulders tense up. "I need to speak to you both." Jessica looked concerned, while Abby looked putout that she had been taken away from whatever she had been doing. "Reporters from the tabloid, 'The Voice' have been in contact with me."

"They have called here also," Jessica admitted.

"My concern is who could have told them that we have separated. Did you tell anyone?" he inquired.

"I did not say a word to anyone," Jessica told him. She looked at him with wet eyes. "I don't think I could get the words out."

Travis nodded. *I did not think she was the one responsible. She would not betray me,* he thought, feeling vindicated. Travis glanced over at Abby. *And neither would Abby.* "Honey, did you say anything to anybody about your mother and me separating? If you did it's alright. I won't be mad at you."

Abby looked directly at her father. "Yeah, I did tell someone. I told James Wilson."

No, thought Travis. "Why did you do that?"

"Because, I hate you! You ruined my life! And I'll never forgive either of you!" she hopped off the couch and ran upstairs.

"Abby!" Jessica cried out in shock and anger. She turned to look at Travis. "I didn't know she did it."

"I didn't either."

Jessica touched his arm in a comforting gestured. "She doesn't hate you, Travis. She is just really hurt and upset right now. She really does love you."

"I can tell."

"Travis, this is not an easy time for her right now. She is upset over all this. Just give her some time." She pushed a strand of hair out of her face and looked at him with concern in her eyes. "What are you going to do about the press?"

"Brad said he would work on it."

"Just keep Abby out of whatever the two of you do."

"I will. I won't use her. Or you." He got up from the couch and headed toward the door. "I better go. I have work I need to do. And you need to check on Abby."

Jessica followed him to the door. *You should come with me to check on her,* she thought. But she knew that saying that to him would not do any good so instead she said, "Travis, I do hope that you and Brad can put some kind of spin on this situation."

"Thanks, Jess," he said. Travis thought going with Jessica to check on Abby, but decided against it. He would probably just make things worse. She shut the door behind him. He sighed sadly and headed for his car.

Meanwhile, Jessica was going up the stairs. She barged into Abby's room. "What were you thinking, Abby? I can't believe you betrayed your father and me like this."

Abby shrugged her shoulders. She did not really care what her mother thought. She had wanted to hurt them as much as they had hurt her. And it had worked. She picked up a Seventeen magazine up from the floor and began to flip through it.

Jessica yanked it out of her hands. "Don't ignore me when I am talking to you young lady! I want to know why you called, 'The Voice.'"

Abby glared at her mother. "You want to know why? Well, I'll tell you why." She got up from the bed and stood in front of her mother. Abby looked at her mother straight in the eye. "Because, no one cares about my feelings. No asked me if I wanted Dad to move out. No one..." she drifted off as she fought back tears.

"Abby," Jessica tried to put her arms around her, but Abby pushed her away.

"Don't say you are doing what is best for me, because I don't believe it." Abby ran out of her room. She had to get out of the house. She had to get away from all this stress and pressure. The one place she knew she could do that was Michael's.

She drove to Michael's small apartment on the other side of town. When she arrived at his apartment building she did not see his motorcycle. Frustrated, Abby sped off. *To tell the truth I am glad he was not home. I did not really want to see him. I just came here because it would piss Mom and Dad off,* she admitted to herself, *Like calling the tabloid did.* Abby began to feel a little bit guilty over what she had done.

Abby headed back into the city. Before going home she decided to visit her father. She wanted to talk to him. Tell him how much he had let her down. Abby pulled into the Rosemont Hotel parking lot. She got out of her car and went into the lobby. She walked up to the information desk. The man behind the desk put the newspaper down. "May, I help you?"

"I would like Senator Moore's room, please."

"And you are?" he asked in a snotty voice. He looked at her over his reading glasses. His eyes roamed down her. He took in her tight black pants and off the shoulder green sweater. He raised a prim eyebrow. She knew what he was thinking.

"I am his daughter, Abby."

"One moment." He picked up the phone. Abby realized he was calling to see if she was really who she said she was. He hung up and turned back to Abby. "You can go up now. You'll have to show the security officer a picture I.D."

Abby headed to the impressive stairway and went up to the first floor. As she walked toward her father's room, Abby reached into her purse and pulled out her wallet. There was a tall muscular African American in a dark blue suit standing outside of Travis's room. He nodded at her when she approached him. "Hello, miss."

"I am here to see my father," she told him.

"I'll need to see some form of I.D." She could see a sting of doubt in the guard's eyes. He looked her over. He probably thought it was some kind of prank. No senator's daughter would dress like that. Especially, one whose father was running for president.

The door opened and Travis stuck his head out. "It's alright, Joe." He came out of the room. "This is my daughter Abby."

Joe gave her a slight smile. "Nice to meet you."

"Nice to meet you, too," she told him, putting her wallet back in her purse. She was glad she did not have show him her I.D. It was not a good picture of her. She would have been embarrassed to show it to such a good-looking guy.

"Joe, I don't want to be disturbed. My daughter and I have something we need to discuss." He took Abby's arm and pulled her into the hotel room.

"Yes, sir."

Abby stepped into the luxurious room. She sat down on the neatly made bed. Travis gave her a big smile as he sat down in the chair across from her. He was thrilled that she had come to see him. "I am glad you came to see me. I know things haven't been to good between us." The phone rang and Travis sighed in frustration. "Just a minute, honey." He picked up the phone.

Probably, be something that is important and he'll have to go and take care of it. Everything is more important than me, she thought feeling hurt. *Well, screw him.* She was not going to wait around for him. She had been willing to work things out, but not now. Abby jumped up from the bed and ran out the door.

"Abby!" Travis yelled after her. He hung the phone up and ran after her. When he got outside she was getting in her car. Tires squealed as she sped off. Travis hurried over to his car and went after her. He sped after her. His heart was pounding as he chased her. *She going to get herself killed,* he thought.

About a mile up the road Travis saw Abby turn into the Cherub's a bar that was known for serving alcohol to minors. He pulled into the parking lot and went into the bar. The smell of cigarette smoke and stale beer overwhelmed him. It was empty except for Abby and the bar tender. Abby was sitting at the bar. "Abby!"

She turned around and glared at him. "Why did you follow me?" she had a beer in her hand.

Travis ignored her question as he walked to the bar. "Don't do this, Abby. You nearly killed yourself the last time you drank."

"Like you care."

"I care more than you'll ever know, Abby." He sat down on the stool next to hers. "I know that what's been going on has not been easy on you. But this is not the answer." He indicated to the mug of beer she had in her hand.

"Miss, is this guy bothering you?" the beefy bartender asked coming over to Abby and Travis.

Travis turned and fixed his angry glare on the barkeep. "No, I am not bothering her. I am her father."

"It's alright. He's my father," she agreed.

Travis continued to stare at the man behind the bar. "I have a question for you, pal. How do you sleep at night after getting minors drunk? Do you care that they can get themselves killed?"

"Hey, it's not my fault if they drink and drive."

Travis stood up and reached across the bar and grabbed the man by the collar of his grungy shirt. "Why you bastard..." he drew back a fist.

Abby grabbed his arm to keep him from punching the guy. She was shocked. She knew that her father had a temper, but she never saw him hit someone before. It kind of scared her. "Dad, don't. He's not worth it."

"Get out both of you. Before I call the cops!" The bartender ordered.

He did not have to tell Abby and Travis twice. They hurried out of the bar. Travis walked Abby to her car. Before getting into the car she turned to him. "Thank you for coming after me. You didn't have to."

"You're my daughter. Despite what you think I would do anything for you."

Abby meet her father's eyes with her own. "Dad, I am sorry about calling, 'The Voice.' I know it was the wrong thing to do. I just wanted to hurt you and Mom. I am really sorry that I did it."

Travis gave her a hug and was delighted when Abby hugged him back. "I know you are sorry. And I forgive you." He put a hand on her cheek. "I am sorry for everything too, Abby."

Abby pulled away and tucked her hair behind her ear. "Thanks, Dad." She could tell that he was still upset. "Dad, are you okay?"

Travis looked over his shoulder at Cherub's and then back at Abby. "Yeah, I am fine," he said unconvincingly. "We should get you home. Your mother is going to be worried about you."

Abby got into her car and Travis got into his and they drove to the house. Abby called her mother on her cell phone to let her know that she fine and that she was on her way home.

Jessica was waiting for them when they pulled up to the house. She ran out to Abby's car. She threw her arms around Abby. "Honey, I was so worried," she cried.

"I am sorry, Mom. Really sorry." She pulled away from her.

"I know you are, Abby." She hugged her daughter again. "Go inside and we will talk more in a minute."

"Okay," Abby said, and went inside the house.

Jessica gave Travis a hug. "Thank you."

"For what?" he asked, hugging her back.

"For taking care of her."

Travis gave her a small smile. "She is my daughter. I'll always take care of her."

Jessica pulled away. *He is still upset. There is something else bothering him. He is not just upset about Abby,* she thought. "Are you okay?" Travis nodded and told her that he was, although he was not sure.

Chapter Six

A week later Abby was walking through her school parking lot toward the high school. Things were getting better between her and her parents. She was disappointed that Jessica and Travis had not reunited after her father brought her home from Cherub's. But there was nothing she could do about that. She looked around the parking lot. She could have sworn she heard someone call out her name. Kids rushed past her as the hurried toward the school. A few of them would wave at her, but did not approach her.

"Abby!" she heard the male voice again. She turned around and saw Michael Kinkade running up to her. He was wearing a pair of dirty jeans and a black shirt that had a hole in the side. "Hey, Abby-girl."

Abby was not happy to see him. She had been able to avoid him for days. She adjusted the strap of her book bag. "What do you want, Michael?"

"I just wanted to see you. I have not seen you in a while. What's up?" he asked her. He leaned over to kiss her, but she moved her head back. "What's going on?"

"Michael, it's over." She headed toward the school. Abby wanted to get away from Michael as fast as possible.

Michael grabbed her arm and yanked her back. "What do you mean it's over?"

Abby jerked her arm free of his grasp. "It means that I don't want to see you again, Mike."

Michael Kinkade grabbed her arm again and pulled her close. "You better think twice before you dump me. I know things about you that your father wouldn't want the press to get a hold of. I can destroy you and your family, " he warned.

"Who would believe you? After all you gave an underage girl alcohol. You slept with a minor. Go ahead go to the press. The D.A. would love it. He would have a full confession."

Michael laughed a cruel laugh. "I am not worried. I would just pass myself off as a concerned ex-boyfriend. I would just want to tell the voters of America the truth about the Moore family. They deserve to know the whole story." He rubbed his chin with a hand. "I can just see the headlines now. Poor Travis won't stand a chance."

"Go to hell," she spat. She turned and ran toward the school.

"One of us is going to hell, Abby, but it won't be me!" Michael yelled at her. Michael pulled out his cell phone and hit the memory button. "Hello? Is this 'The Voice,' newspaper office?" he waited a second. "It is? Good." He watched as Abby hurried into the school. *No one dumps me and gets away with it,* he thought revengefully. "I have a story that I think you'll be interested in." Michael gave a wicked smile. "Let's just say I am a concerned citizen." *It's payback time.*

* * * * * * * * * * *

Later that evening Travis was getting ready for a fundraiser. He finished buttoning his shirt when there was a knock on the door. "Come in!" he said. His aide Kevin came in. "Hi, Kevin."

"Senator," he said seriously.

Travis gave a weak smile. *He always sounds serious. I don't think I have heard him laugh or smile,* he thought. "Are you ready for the fundraiser?" He bent over and tied his shoes.

"We have a problem," Kevin said.

Travis sat up from tying his shoes and looked at the younger man concerned. "What is it, Kevin? Is there a problem with the fundraiser?"

Kevin handed him a copy of, 'The Voice.' "They ran this as a special edition."

Travis looked confused at Kevin and took the paper. He read the headline and groaned. *No, not that,* he thought. Travis read half the story and was disgusted. "Damn it!" He threw the paper on the table.

Kevin looked concerned. "What are you going to do, Senator? Should I call Senator Johnson for you?"

"No, I'll take care of it." He looked at the newspaper headline that glared out to be noticed.

The Voice
Presidential Candidate daughter is an alcoholic.

* * * * * * * * * * * *

Jessica tossed the tabloid in the trashcan and looked over at Abby. "Your dad is not going to be happy about this." She rubbed her temples and sat down on the couch.

"Do you think he knows about the article?" Abby came out of the kitchen carrying a glass of water and an sprain. She handed her mother the pill and water.

Jessica popped the pill in her mouth and swallowed some water. "It is a safe bet that he does. When he saw it he probably blew a fuse."

"This is all my fault," Abby said. "I am such a screw up."

"You are not a screw up, Abby." The bell rang and Jessica sighed. *Perfect,* she thought. She got up from the couch and went to the front door. She opened the door and was stunned to see Travis in a tux. "Travis! Come in!" she smiled as he entered the house. She had always loved how he looked in a tuxedo. *He looks so sexy in that tux,* she thought to herself. The tux fit his form perfectly. It brought out his dark blue eyes, which she loved. His salt and pepper hair laid in a wave and looked like it had been mused down.

"Did you see the paper?" he asked, breaking into her thoughts.

"Yes," she admitted with a blush. Her smile fell from her lips. "Abby and I were just talking about it. Abby is pretty upset over it."

"I want to see Abby." He walked into the family room where Abby was sitting. He sat down next to her and gave her a hug. "Are you okay?"

"I am fine, Dad. I am just sorry that Michael did this." She looked at her parents with tears in her eyes. "You guys were right. In the end Michael did hurt me. And he hurt you guys, too." She got up from the couch. "I want to be alone for a while. I'll be in my room." She did not go upstairs she sat down on the landing where her parents could not see her. She wanted to know what they were going to say each other.

Jessica sat down where Abby had been sitting a second ago. "I am worried about her. She has been depressed all evening."

"I hate that she had to go through this."

"Me, too."

Travis patted her hand and gave her a comforting smile. "But she will get through this. And so will you. This will die down in a few days."

Jessica jerked her hand away from his touch. "Don't patronize me, Travis. This is not going to go away over night." She folded her arms across her chest so he could not touch them again. "There are going to be more stories and rumors. Do you think that is fair to her?"

Travis looked at his watch. He could not spend the night arguing with Jessica. "I have to go. I have a fundraiser tonight. We'll talk about this later."

Abby sighed sadly and got up from the step and went to her room.

"Fine. I don't want to keep you," Jessica snapped. She got up and went up stairs. And Travis stormed out of the house.

* * * * * * * * * * * *

Two months later Jessica knew there was something physically wrong with her. She had been feeling sick and run down for the last couple of weeks. At thirty-eight, she thought she was going through menopause. But there was a seed of doubt in her mind that it was not menopause causing her poor health. That morning she had gone to the drugstore and bought a home pregnancy test. She had hoped no one had seen her. The last thing she wanted was rumors going around about her. *It won't be positive, it won't be,* she thought to herself. These were turning into the longest five minutes of her life. She tried looking through magazines, but she could not concentrate on them. The timer on her nightstand finally went off and she went into the bathroom.

She went to the sink where the pregnancy test sat. Jessica read the instruction to the test again. "A negative sign you are not pregnant," she read. "A plus sign you are pregnant." *Well, it's going to be negative. There is no way that I can be pregnant,* she thought, trying to convince herself. Jessica picked up the test and almost dropped it when she saw the results. It showed the plus sign.

Jessica's knees buckled and she fell. *I am pregnant,* she thought. "No, it can't be." She looked at the test again with its plus sign glaring at her. Jessica remembered a day a couple of months ago when she and Travis had made love. They had not used any protection. Jessica angrily threw the pregnancy test in the trashcan. She buried her face in her hands. *What am I going to do?* She thought despondently.

"Mom?" Jessica heard Abby knock on her bedroom door. "Mom, breakfast is ready." She could hear Abby walk away from the door and go back downstairs. Jessica started sobbing. *This can't be happening. Not now,* she thought in agony. She cried for several minutes. She finally calmed herself down. Jessica got up from the floor and washed any sign of her crying off her face. She did not want to tell Abby the news just yet. She went downstairs to the kitchen.

Abby was at the table eating a couple of slices of French toast. She looked up when she saw her mother come in. "How are you feeling, Mom?" She knew that her mother had not been feeling well. Abby was starting to get concerned. She wished her mother would open up to her about what was wrong.

Jessica swallowed hard and felt nauseous as the smell of French toast hit her. "I feel fine," she lied.

Abby got up from her chair and went to the stove. "Do you want some French toast?"

Jessica felt her stomach churn. She knew that she was going to throw up. She hurried to the trashcan. She threw off the lid and leaned over and vomited.

Abby rushed to her mother's side. She held Jessica's hair back as she finished. She gagged herself, but was grateful that she did not throw up. Abby rubbed her mother's back as she heaved. "Are you okay now, Mom?" she asked, and handed her a paper towel.

Jessica wiped her mouth. "No."

Abby felt her heart go cold with fear. "What's wrong?"

Jessica decided to tell Abby the truth. She was not going to be able to hide it from her. "I am pregnant."

"What?"

"I am pregnant," Jessica repeated. She sat down at the table. She pushed Abby's plate away from her. The smell of French toast was making her feel sick again. "I just took a pregnancy test and it was positive."

Abby was stunned. "Is it Dad's?"

Jessica was offended. "Yes, it is. I must be about two months pregnant."

Abby sat down at the table across from her mother. *Wow, this is big. Really big. I always wanted a brother or sister,* she thought in awe. "Are you going to keep the baby?"

Jessica put her head in her hands. That had been a question she had been asking herself since she thought she might be pregnant. "I don't know. I am thirty-eight years old, Abby. This is not going to be an easy pregnancy. Plus, the baby could have birth defects. And not to mention that my marriage is in shambles."

"I'll be here to help you."

"Abby…"

"Mom, you have taken care of me for the last sixteen years."

Jessica reached across the table and took Abby's hands in hers. "That is my job. You don't have to feel like you have to baby-sit me." She gave Abby a kiss on her forehead.

"Are you going to tell Dad? He needs to know," Abby told her mother.

Jessica sighed, she knew that whatever she decided to do about the baby, Travis would need to know. "I'll talk to him tomorrow." Travis was going want to do the noble thing and move back home. She got up from the chair. "I am tired. I think I'll take a nap."

"I'll check on you later," Abby promised.

Jessica did not say anything. If checking on her made Abby feel better she would go ahead and let her do it. To tell the truth it made her feel better knowing that Abby was there.

* * * * * * * * * * * *

Travis was stretched out on his bed reading a badly written western novel. He felt his eyelids droop. He shook himself awake and tried to read some more of the book. But again his eyes closed and the book fell to the floor. He moaned and rolled his head from side to side on the pillow. "No."

Travis thrashed around on his bed. "No!" he screamed, and sat up in bed. Sweat had soaked his shirt and covered his face. He drew his knees up to his chest and put his head on his knees. He took deep gulping breaths to calm himself. Travis shut his eyes and he could see the fireball again. He clutched his head in his hands. "Why do I have to remember?"

<u>Chapter Seven</u>

Abby watched as her mother collapsed onto the couch. Jessica laid down and put a wet cloth to her forehead. "I feel awful," she told Abby. "When I was pregnant with you, I did not have any morning sickness. But with this pregnancy, I am sick all the time."

Abby put her Stephen King book down and gave her mother a sympathetic look. "Can I get you anything? Do you want some 7-Up or saltines? They might help your stomach."

Jessica swallowed hard and rubbed her stomach. "I don't think so, Abby. I don't think I can keep anything down." She gave her a faint smile. "Thanks anyway."

Abby she got up from the chair and walked to the couch. She sat down by her mother's feet. "Are you going to tell Dad about the baby today?" she inquired.

Jessica felt her stomach turn against her; she prayed that she would not throw up. Maybe, some of her stomach problems were associated with her worries about telling Travis that she was pregnant. "I don't know."

Abby was about to say something else when the doorbell rang. Jessica tried to get up, but Abby held up a hand. "I'll answer it. I'll tell whoever it is to go away." Jessica nodded.

Abby hurried to the door. She opened the door and there was Travis. He looked exhausted. "Hi, Dad."

Travis gave her a strained smile and a quick kiss on the cheek. "Hi, honey. Why aren't you in school?"

"I don't have to be there till noon."

"Oh," he let out a yawn. "I need to see your mother for a minute. Is she home?"

Abby looked over her shoulder to the living room where Jessica was. She knew that her mother did not want any visitors, but this was her father. Abby decided to let him see her. She moved aside so he could enter the house. "She is not feeling too good. But she'll be glad to see you," Abby told him.

"I won't stay to long," Travis promised, and followed Abby into the living room.

Jessica was sitting up on the couch her hands were on her stomach. "I wish I this morning sickness would go away," she muttered, as Abby and Travis came into the living room.

"Jessica?"

Jessica looked up when she heard his voice. She saw Travis staring at her in shock. His face was turning white and she could see the confusion growing in his eyes. She knew that he had heard her. She looked over at Abby. "Would you excuse us for a minute?" she asked. Abby trotted up the stairs. Jessica then turned to her husband. *This is not how I wanted to tell him,* she thought. "Travis, there is something I need to tell you."

"I know what you are going to say. You are pregnant. I heard you a minute ago talking about morning sickness." He gave her an accusing look. "Who is the father?" he demanded.

Jessica met his dark blue eyes. They were filled with hurt. "You are. Remember that day a couple of months back when we made love? Abby had just been released from the hospital."

Travis remembered that day well. "We are going to have a baby," he whispered in shock. Travis walked over to the big picture window and looked out. "When were you going to tell me? When the baby was born?" his voice trembled.

"Travis, I haven't known that long."

He continued to stare out the window. He could not face her. Travis could not believe that she had kept this from him. "The minute you found out that you were pregnant you should have told me."

"It has been quite a shock to me," she explained. "I have not been able to process it yet."

Travis nodded. He could understand that. He was feeling the same way. He finally turned around and looked at her. "Are you happy about the baby?" he asked. Travis was not sure he wanted to know the answer.

Jessica felt her eyes fill with tears. *This should be one the happiest moments of my life but its not,* she thought sadly. "Travis, I don't know if I am going to have this baby."

Travis stormed over to her. "What do you mean?"

"I have been thinking about having an abortion."

"No."

Jessica sighed. She knew that he would not look at the big picture. "Travis...

"I said no. I won't let you kill my baby."

Jessica sucked in a couple of calming breaths. She had to explain her fears to him, "Travis, this baby could have all kinds of health problems. And this would be difficult pregnancy."

"Have you been to a doctor?" he wanted to know. "Well, have you Jessica?"

"No."

"So where are you getting your medical advise? Off a cereal box? Let's talk to a doctor. Let's see what they say." Travis put his hands on her shoulders and looked deeply into her green eyes. "Please, give this baby a chance."

Jessica burst into tears. She felt herself being pulled into his arms. She buried her face in his chest. Tears stained his gray shirt. Travis ran a hand up and down her back. She was scared. She had lied when she told Travis that she had wanted a abortion. That was the furthest thing from the truth. She did want the baby. She finally calmed down and pulled away from him. "We'll talk to the doctor."

"Good." *I hope she says yes,* he thought. Travis could feel the butterflies in his stomach. "I think I should move back home."

"I don't think that would be a good idea."

"You don't think that would be a good idea? Why not?" Travis asked feeling hurt all over again.

"You know why."

"Yeah," he said in a thick voice, "you are trying to shove me out of your life and Abby's life. And you'll do the same thing with this baby."

Jessica sighed feeling frustrated. "No, that's not true. I don't want to think about the election. I don't want reporters here all the time watching me. I just can't deal with all that right now." She put a hand on his check and turned his head toward her. She forced him to meet her gaze. "I want you in my life and in our children's lives. But your career is something that I can't handle right now."

Travis pulled away from her. He paced around the living room. "There's that ultimatum again. I can either have my family or can I have my career. But I can't have them both."

Jessica began to feel sick to her stomach again. She knew that it was not caused by morning sickness. "Travis, I am not doing this now."

Travis glared at her again. "Fine, I'll go. Let me know when the doctor's appointment is." He stormed out of the house.

* * * * * * * * * * * *

Later that night Abby was at Melinda's house where a huge party was beginning held. The party was just getting started when she arrived. Abby looked around the living room. Some of the kids were drinking beer while others were smoking pot. Abby sighed and wondered why she came to the party. "Hi, Abby!" Courtney Miles said, staggering up to her. Abby could tell that she was well on her way to becoming drunk. "Great party, huh?" she slurred.

"Yeah," Abby muttered. She wished that Courtney would go away. "Looks like everyone is having a great time." She watched as Tim Barnes tripped over his own feet. He crashed into the stereo and his friends laughed.

"It's wild." Courtney leaned closer to Abby. She winced as she smelled the alcohol on Courtney's breath. "I heard about you and Michael breaking up. I always thought he was a jerk."

"Thanks," Abby said. She was no longer in the mood to be polite to Courtney anymore. "I'll see you later." She walked off. She never really liked Courtney that much. She just tolerated her.

Abby walked over to the couch and sat down. She thought back to earlier in the day as she listened in on a conversation between her parents. Travis had wanted to move back in, but her mother had turned him down. Abby could not understand why two people who loved one another could not work out their problems. What about love conquers all and all that crap? She had also heard her mother say she was not sure if she was going to have the baby. Abby had been disappointed when she heard that.

Abby thought about the news story about her in the paper. They had called her an alcoholic, but she was not one. She only drank to relax and to have fun. An alcoholic had to drink to function and that was not her. She controlled her desire to drink. Not the other way around. "Hey, Abby!" She turned and saw John Thompson sat down next to her. He handed her a beer. Abby put the beer on the table. She vowed that she was not going to drink. Although every nerve in her body was crying out for the beer. "I saw the article about you in, 'The Voice.' I bet your parents were pissed."

Abby sighed. *Is that all people are going to talk about tonight?* She thought feeling annoyed. "Yeah, they weren't happy about it," she admitted. Abby wished that he would go away. He was starting annoy her.

"Aren't you going to drink your beer? I could get you something else."

"No."

"I saw Michael Kinkande today. He was pretty happy with the article. He told me that they paid him quite a lot for the story. He said he had some other things that he was going to tell them."

Abby felt alarmed at what John had told her. There were a lot of things that she had done that she was ashamed of. She reached over to the table and picked up the beer. She was too shaken up to think straight. She knew that the beer would calm her down and she would be able to think. Plus, with everybody talking about the article in the newspaper she was getting tense. Abby opened the can and took a swallow of beer. She felt herself relax.

John smiled and reached over and tried to fondle her breast. Abby stood up and threw her beer in his face. "Hey!" he cried out. He wiped the beer off his face. John gave her a furious look. "Kinkade was right. You are a bitch."

Abby stalked off. She was not in the mood to deal with a brunch of high, drunken people. She pulled another beer out of the cooler and went to her car. She opened the beer and took a long drink before starting her BMW. She pulled the car out of the driveway and headed to the highway.

Abby squinted out her windshield. Things looked bleary and out of focus. She took a drink of beer and was barely able to stop at a stop sign. "That was close," she said, as a Mac truck zoomed by the front of her car.

Abby pulled out on to the highway. The first thing she heard was the squealing of tires. She heard the collision before she felt anything. She would never forget the sound of crunching metal and breaking glass. The last thing she remembered was her head slamming into the steering wheel.

* * * * * * * * * * *

Jessica sat next to Abby's bed holding her hand. There was a white bandage on her forehead. She had various cuts and bruises on her face and arms. The beep, beep sound of the heart monitor assured her that Abby was alive. Jessica touched Abby's head gently. "Oh, baby. Why did this have to happen?"

Jessica would never forget the call from the police department telling her that there had been accident. For a minute she thought Abby had been killed. She was relieved when they told her that Abby was alive. Jessica was relieved that the people in the other car had been able to walk away from the wreck.

"Jessica?"

Jessica looked toward the door and saw Travis standing there. He came into the room and went to the other side of the bed. "How is she?" he asked sitting down.

"She'll be fine. She just has a concussion."

"Thank God."

"She was drinking. They found a beer can in her car and her blood alcohol level was over the legal limit," Jessica sobbed. She covered her eyes with her free hand. "She promised me she wouldn't drink. She promised me."

Travis did not say anything to her. He was fighting back tears himself. *I have failed her,* he thought to himself. He took her hand and squeezed it.

Jessica calmed herself down. She took the tissues out of the box and wiped her eyes. "I have called the rehab center. We can admit her as soon as she is out of the hospital."

Travis looked at her with anger in his eyes. "You should have talked to me before you consulted them."

"You wouldn't have let me called them. I should have called them when she had alcohol poisoning, but I let you both talk me out of it. Well, not this time. She is going to the rehab clinic," she said in a low determined voice, so not to disturb Abby or the other patients.

"I just don't think she needs to go to a rehab clinic. She was at a party that got out of hand. The people to blame are the parents of the child who had the party."

"Travis, you are not facing reality. She almost killed herself and someone else tonight. She is not just a teenager that is experimenting with alcohol. She has a serious problem. Abby needs more help than what we can give her. She needs to go to a treatment center," Jessica said, a little louder than she intended.

A woman in blue scrubs came to the door. She looked at both of them irritably. "If you two don't quit down, I'll ask you both to leave."

Jessica looked sheepish. She knew that she should not be yelling at Travis in the hospital. But sometimes she felt that was the only way to get him to listen to her. "I am sorry. It won't happen again."

Travis looked at the nurse and gave her an apologetic smile. "I didn't mean to upset anyone."

The nurse rolled her eyes and walked away from the doorway. "Make sure it doesn't happen again."

Jessica sighed and tried to remain calm. "Travis, this is the second time that she has nearly killed herself with alcohol. I am going to admit her into the rehab clinic, rather you approve or not."

Travis got up from the chair and walked to the other side of the room. "Don't I get a say in the decision?"

"Of course you do, Travis. I just want to do what is best for her. I don't want her hurt anymore."

"I would never hurt her."

Jessica looked at him unhappily. "Maybe, you wouldn't hurt her intentionally. But your life is very much in the public eye. They are going scrutinize everything in your life." She looked down at her consciousness daughter. "Abby was already hurt by the press." She looked at him with tears in her eyes. "She has been through enough already."

80

Travis sat down on the empty bed. Maybe, Jessica was right. Maybe, Abby was an alcoholic and needed to go to the rehab clinic. He did not want her to end up like his brother. But he did not want the press to get a hold of this. It could ruin his political career. He would have to be careful. He ran both his hands through his thick hair. He met Jessica's gaze. "I'll do whatever you think is best for Abby."

Jessica went over to Travis and sat down next to him. She looked at his tired face. There were dark circles under his eyes and his gray hair was starting to turn white. There were thin lines around his mouth and his normally sparkling blue eyes were now a dull blue. He had a five o'clock shadow that gave him a rugged look. "Thank you, Travis."

"Oh," came a moan from the bed.

Jessica and Travis looked at the bed and turned to one another. "Did you hear that?" They asked each other at the same time.

"Oh."

They both hurried to the bed. Jessica leaned over the bed and touched Abby face gently. "Abby, baby, can you hear me?" Abby moaned again and she opened her eyes. "Oh, Abby."

"Mom," Abby said. She saw her father hovering over her as well. "Dad, I am sorry." She whispered weakly.

Jessica sat down on the bed and took Abby's hand in hers. "Abby, how do you feel? Are you in any pain?"

Abby let a couple of tears slip out. "I am sorry," she said again. "I am sorry for everything."

Travis leaned over and gave her a kiss on her forehead. "It's alright honey."

Abby pulled away from her father's touch. *They were right. I do have a problem. I almost killed someone last night,* she realized. Abby looked back at her mother and met her green eyes with her own. "I need help." She looked over at her father. "Please, help me."

* * * * * * * * * * * *

Three days later Abby was well enough to transferred to the treatment center. Travis had decided that it would be best if he stayed from the clinic. He had heard second hand that Abby had settled in the clinic easily. She would be in the clinic for a month. Travis sighed. *I should have been there today,* he thought to himself, *but I just couldn't bring myself to do it.*

He got up from the bed and went to his closet. He pulled out a pinstriped suite out and tossed it on the bed. He was not in the mood for tonight's town hall meeting.

He quickly changed out of his jeans and t-shirt and into the suite. He was putting on his tie when there was a knock at the door. "Come in!" he yelled out. His campaign manger came in. "Hi, Brad. I'll be ready to go in a minute."

Brad, who was dressed similarly to Travis, sat his brief case on the table. "Don't be in any hurry. We need to go over the recent Gallop Poll numbers." He opened his briefcase and pulled out a couple pieces of paper and handed them to Travis. "You are not going to be happy about this." Travis took the paper from him and looked at them. "You are down in the polls, Travis. You are about twenty points behind Stuart O'Neil," Brad explained mentioning the other democratic contender for president.

"O'Neil has not been firm on the issues! All he has done is make promises that will never work once in office."

"Women voters just don't see you as a family man. You need to be seen more with Abby and Jessica."

Travis squeezed his eyes shut and rubbed them with his fingers. "Jessica would never agree to that. And you know that Abby is in the rehab clinic. Even if she were here, I would never use her like that." He handed the papers back to Brad.

"Travis, you are taking a stand on the issues and that is striking a cord with the male voters. But you are not making a connection to the female because you are not with your family." Brad sat down in of the cushy chairs.

Travis began to pace around his hotel room. "What should I do? Force Jessica to take me back so I can win the election?"

Brad watched him as he paced back and forth in front of him. "You have told me many times before that you wanted to reunite with Jessica. So find away to do it."

He makes it sound so simple, Travis thought as he continued to pace. "She'll just think that I am using her to win the election." He stopped in front of the window and looked out at the busy Washington D.C. street.

"You can't let her know that that's what you are doing. Just say that you want to be a family again. Do everything that she wants you to do. And once the two of you are together again, you'll go up in the polls." Brad put the papers back in his brief case and shut it.

"You mean trick her? I couldn't do that to Jessica."

Brad got up and yanked the briefcase off the table and gave a frustrated sigh. "Do you want to be president?"

"Yes."

"Do you want your family back?"

"You know that I do."

"Then do what you have to do to get both." Brad walked to the door. "But you better do it quickly or you'll lose the election." He opened the door and glanced over

83

at Travis. "I am going to go on to the high school and make sure everything is all set up."

"Okay, I'll be there soon."

"Think about what I have said." Brad went out the door.

Travis sat down at the desk and picked up a framed picture of Jessica. He smiled at it as he gently touched her face. "I love you, Jessica," he said. He continued to gaze lovingly at the picture. "What are we going to do?" Travis put the picture back down on the desk. He propped his elbows up on the desk and put his head in hands. "What am I going to do?"

Chapter Eight

"Thank you for coming with me, Travis. I didn't want to come here alone," Jessica told Travis a week later. They were sitting in Dr. Morgan's waiting room. It was a Monday so the obstetrician office was full.

Travis took her hand and gave it a comforting squeeze. "Of course I would come with you. This is my baby, too."

Jessica squeezed his hand back. This was her first visit to the doctors. With everything that had been going on, she had not had the time to go before. She glanced around the room. The women that were waiting were in various stages of pregnancy. Most of them were there with their husbands, but there were two of them by themselves. They all looked young enough to be her daughter. She felt herself blush with embarrassment. She looked over at Travis. He was tapping his foot quickly. Jessica smiled. That was a sign that he was either nervous or uncomfortable. Jessica could not help but smile.

Travis looked over at Jessica. "How are you doing?"

"I am scared," she admitted. "What if there is something wrong with the baby?" she put a hand on her stomach. Once she had gotten over the initial shock she was happy about the baby. She wanted this baby. But she was terrified that there was something wrong with her child.

Travis put an arm around her shoulder and pulled her close. "Hey, don't talk like that. The baby is going to be fine. We are going to have a healthy baby."

Jessica looked at him hopefully. "Promise?"

"I promise," he hoped that he was right.

Jessica was about to respond when a dark headed woman in green scrubs came down the hall. She was holding a clipboard in her hand reading it. She looked up when she came into the waiting room. "Jessica? Jessica Moore?"

Jessica stood up. "That's me," she told the nurse. She looked over at Travis. "Come with me."

Travis looked at the nurse. "Is it alright if I go back with her?"

The nurse nodded and gave them a warm smile. "Of course you can." She led them down the hall that she had come up from. She looked over at Jessica. "Is this your first time here?"

"Yes," was all she could say.

The nurse did not seem to notice. She had seen plenty of nervous people come through. She had Jessica get on the scale and got her weight and height. She then led them back to a small exam room. The nurse quickly took Jessica's temperature and blood pressure. She then handed Jessica a hospital gown. "Put this on and I'll be right back." She stepped out of the little room.

Jessica looked over at Travis. She did not want him in the room while she changed. "Uh, Travis could you go outside too?"

If Travis's feelings were hurt he did not let on. He went out the door. Jessica quickly changed into the hospital gown. She folded her clothes and put them on the chair at the far end of the exam room. Jessica stared at the diplomas and wondered why doctors had to have their degrees on display. Was it because they wanted to prove they were really doctors? Jessica did not know. She opened the door and told Travis he could come back in.

"The nurse had to check on another patient," he explained, as he entered the room.

Jessica sat down on the exam table and watched as Travis took the chair that was next to the metal desk. "Travis, the reason I asked you to step out a minuet ago was my..."

"You don't have to explain, Jess. I understand."

"I don't feel attractive right now," she said embarrassed. "I feel bloated and I didn't want you to see me like that."

"I think you are beautiful," he told her.

She was about to reply to him when a woman a little older than Jessica came into the room. She had a lab coat on and a nametag that read Josie Morgan Ob-gyn on it. She was tall and slender. Her gray hair was pulled up into a high ponytail. She gave them a welcoming smile. She shook hands with Jessica first. "This must be the mother-to-be. I am Doctor Morgan."

"I am Jessica Moore." She indicated to Travis. "This is my husband Travis."

Dr. Morgan shook hands with Travis and turned her attention back to Jessica. She flipped through the file and muttered to herself, "Thirty-eight years old, about three months pregnant." She checked the vitals that the nurse had taken. "Blood pressure and temperature look good." She closed the file and set it on her desk. Dr. Morgan helped Jessica lay back on the table. "This is going to be the least enjoyable part of the visit. I need to do a pelvic exam."

Jessica held out a hand to Travis and he took it. She grasped it tightly as the doctor poked and prodded her. She closed her eyes tightly and pretended she was anywhere but there. She whimpered and Travis stroked her cheek with the back of his hand. He whispered in her ear that she was doing great.

After Dr. Morgan was done with the exam she pushed the stool back and snapped off her rubber gloves. "That wasn't so bad now was it?"

Jessica did not answer her. She could not give an honest answer to her question. Besides, she had more important things on her mind. Like her baby. "Is everything alright with my baby?"

Dr. Morgan gave her a motherly smile. "From what I can tell today everything looks good," she became serious. "But with your age I am going to want to monitor you closely."

"Okay."

Dr. Morgan opened the file again. She made some notes and looked at them. "I am going to want to see you in a few weeks for an ultrasound."

Jessica looked over at Travis. "Is that you okay with you?"

"Yes," he told her. He would keep that day open.

"Do you have any questions for me?" Jessica and Travis shook their heads no. "Okay, then. I'll see you in a couple of weeks. Call me if you need me sooner." She left the examination room.

Travis stepped out of the room and waited for Jessica to get dressed. *Thank God that Jessica and the baby are alright. I don't know what I would have done if I had lost either of them,* he thought to himself. Jessica came out of the room. "I am relieved over what Dr. Morgan told us."

"Me, too. I have been so worried about the baby." She rubbed her tummy. "I should have known that the baby was going to be alright."

Travis smiled and embraced her. "I have been worried about the two of you." He let her go. He was not ready to leave her company yet. "Would you like to go to lunch with me?" he asked, feeling like he was asking her out for the first time.

Jessica returned his smile. "Sure." She led toward the check out desk. "The baby must want Chinese for lunch. I have a craving for Chinese."

Travis laughed, "Well, I don't want to deprive my child of Chinese food when he wants it."

"He? Don't you mean she?" She laughed as she stopped at the desk. *It feels good to laugh with him again. If only it would last,* she thought. "I need to make an appointment for an ultrasound."

It took a few minutes to get an appointment hammered out. They walked out to their cars. Travis turned to Jessica, "Do want to ride with me?"

"Sure," she said, climbing into his Mercedes.

He got into the driver seat and looked over at her. "I need to stop at the hotel for a minute."

Jessica nodded. She leaned back in her chair and enjoyed the ride. It felt wonderful to be with Travis without the usual hostilities between them. After twenty minutes Travis pulled into the parking lot and not a minute to soon. Jessica was in dire need of the bathroom. They hurried to Travis's hotel room. Travis opened the door and they went in. "Oh hi, Brad," he said, wondering why he was there. "I didn't know you were going to be here." He waved a hand in Jessica's direction. "You remember my wife, Jessica."

"Hello, Mrs. Moore. Nice to see you again," Brad Johnson said.

"Nice to see you too, Senator," Jessica said, as she rushed to the bathroom.

Travis went to his desk and began to shuffle through the papers on his desk. "Brad, where are those figures on unemployment? I can't seem to find them."

Brad took the paper off the cabinet and handed it to Travis. "You put it up there yesterday."

"Thanks," he said, taking it from him and laid it on his desk. "I'll look at them when I get back from lunch." He signed some papers and tossed the pen back on the desk.

"By the way," Brad said, as Jessica came out of the bathroom. "I have something to show you." He handed Travis a vanilla envelope.

"What is this?" Travis demanded, taking it from him.

"Just a little something that is going to turn the tide in your favor, Travis. Just think of what the voters are going to think when they see these pictures."

Travis opened the envelope and pulled out the pictures. Jessica looked over Travis's shoulder and saw the pictures. They were of Stuart O'Neil and a woman that she knew was not his wife. And they were not discussing politics. "What are you going to do with those pictures?"

"We are going to have them published in, 'The Voice.' Just imagine the fuss that they will cause. Just like that story about Abby did," Brad explained to her.

Jessica was not going to accept that explanation. "You aren't really going to have those pictures published are you?" she asked Travis

"Jessica, this is politics…"

Jessica backed up. She could not believe that Travis was actually going to have those pictures published. "Don't say anything to me. Those pictures are disgusting. I can't believe that you are going to actually use them." She felt something that she never thought she would feel for Travis; disgust. She could not believe that he would do something so under handed. *I don't know who you are anymore,* she thought despondently. "I can't believe you are going to use these!" she cried.

Travis took a step to her. "Jessica, calm down."

"You have said over and over again that you would never resort to mud slinging to win an election. But that was a lie. You'll do anything to get what you want." She wiped the tears off her face. "No matter who gets hurt in the process." Travis did not answer her. "I have to get away from here!" she made her way to the door.

Travis was right after her. He grabbed her by the arm. "Jessica…"

She wrenched her arm out of his grasp. "Don't touch me." She opened the door and stormed out of the hotel room.

Travis knew better than to go after her. He sat down on the bed and felt his heart break. He had come close to having Jessica, but he had blown it.

* * * * * * * * * * * *

A month later Abby returned home from rehab. She was determined to put her life back together. The first thing she was going to do was get caught up with her schoolwork. She pulled her English book out of her book bag and a flyer fell out. She picked it up and read it, National Literature Contest. Abby remembered her English teacher talking about it. Any student that entered would get fifteen bonus points. She pulled out a piece of paper out of her notebook. After all, bonus points were bonus points.

* * * * * * * * * * *

Three weeks later Abby and her parents were at the school auditorium. "I am not going to win," she muttered, to them under her breath. "I don't know why I had to come." She sank lower into her chair.

"Don't talk like that, sweetie," Jessica said, patting her on the shoulder. She tried to get comfortable in the chair, but could not do it. Her back ached all the time and she could feel that her feet were swollen. Jessica looked around the auditorium. It was filling up quickly with students and their parents. "I am sure they are as nervous as you are."

Abby ignored her mother. She gave her father a smile. Abby had been bowled over when Travis told her that he would be able to attend. She thought he would have been too busy with the election to show up. "I am glad you could come."

"I wouldn't have missed it for the world," he told her returning her smile. "I haven't been able to read your story yet, but I am sure it is good."

"Big surprise," Jessica said under her breath.

Travis narrowed his eyes at her. "What did you say?"

Abby exhaled noisily. She thought that they could get through one day without an argument. "Please, don't start," she begged.

Jessica felt bad. She knew that this was a big day for her and she did not want it ruined by her parents arguing. So she decided to ignore Travis. She put her arm around Abby and gave her a squeeze. "Win or lose I am proud of you."

"So am I."

Jessica glared at him, but did not say anything. She was still mad at him. Although she was relieved that she had not seen the pictures of O'Neil and the hooker in the paper. Maybe, common sense had prevailed.

"Ladies and gentlemen may I have your attention, please." Principal Tirey said, from the stage. He waited till he everyone's attention. He gave them a welcoming smile. He ran a hand through his thin disheveled hair trying to straighten it, but it just messed it up more. "I want to say from the start that I am proud of all the students who participated in the literature contest." He paused as the crowd politely applauded. "This was a hard decision for the judges to make. But only three students could be chosen to go on to the finals in New York."

"Wow," Abby uttered in awe.

"Will the following students please join me on stage. James Mc Knight, Connie Roberts, and Abigail Moore."

Abby turned red with embarrassment and got up from her chair. Jessica moved out of the way so she could join the rest of the winners on the stage. Once she reached the stage Connie gave her a hug. "Congratulations," she told both of them.

"James Mc Knight won for the short story, 'Realizing the Dream,' Connie Roberts for the poem, 'The Storm,' and Abigail Moore submitted the short story, 'The Loss.' They will go to New York to compete at the National Contest. Good luck to all three." Principal Tirey shook hands with the three them. He handed each of them a plaque. Then they posed to have their pictures taken before they were able to return to their seats.

Jessica got up and hugged Abby. "I am so proud of you!"

"I can't believe I won!"

Jessica pulled away from her and gave her a big smile. "Your story was very moving. You deserved to win. You are going to have so much fun in New York!"

Abby let her smile drop. "I can't go to New York."

"Why not?" Travis asked her looking concerned. "Don't you want to go?"

"I do want to go," she told him. Abby looked over at her mother. "But who'll look after Mom? I don't want to leave her by herself for two days."

Travis put an arm around Abby and gave her shoulder a squeeze. "I'll look after your mother."

Jessica glared at both of them. "I don't need a babysitter for goodness sake," she snapped at them. "I can take care of myself for two days."

"I just don't want you to be alone, okay? Nancy is on vacation and you'll be alone in that house. I would feel better if you had someone with you." Abby argued.

"Abby..."

"Either Dad stays with you or I won't go. Simple as that."

Jessica looked into her daughter's eyes. They were filled stubborn determination. She knew that Abby was telling the truth. If Travis did not stay with her over the weekend, she would not go. She did not want Abby to miss out on the opportunity to compete nationally. "You win, Abby." she sighed. "Your dad can stay with me the two days. But don't think anything is going to happen."

Travis gave her a tight smile. "I think you can put up with me for two days."

Abby was relieved. She really was worried about her mother being alone. And despite what her mother said, maybe they would get back together. *Maybe, they'll realize that they still love one another and we'll be a family again,* she thought to herself.

* * * * * * * * * * * *

Friday morning they dropped Abby off at the airport. Jessica wiped her eyes as Travis drove. "I know she'll be gone for only two days, but still...my baby's gone," she whimpered.

Travis nodded he felt the same way. They pulled into their driveway and he parked. He got out of the car and opened up the trunk and pulled out his suitcases. He followed her to the guestroom on the second floor. She opened the door and stepped aside so he could go in. Travis sat the heavy suitcase down on the bed. "Thanks."

"Is this room okay?" she inquired.

"It's fine, Jess. Just fine." He opened this suitcase up and began to unpack.

"I am using the other guest room as a nursery," she explained to him.

"That's great. Maybe, we can work on it some this weekend."

Jessica came further into the bedroom. "You don't have to stay here, Travis. We could just tell Abby that you did. I don't want you to feel obligated to stay here. I know how busy you are with your campaign."

Travis turned around. "I want to be here."

Jessica gave him a smile. "The truth is, I didn't want to be alone."

Travis walked over to her. He could not help himself. He put his arms around her and pulled her close.

Jessica tilted her head back to look at him. His head was coming closer. She could almost taste his sweet kiss. She

95

quickly came to her senses. *I am not ready for this,* Jessica thought in a panic. She jerked away from him. "Travis, don't."

Jessica saw the hurt in his eyes. Travis turned his back to her and went back to his unpacking. "Don't worry, Jessica. I won't force you to do anything you don't want to do."

Chapter Nine

The next morning Travis stood outside of bathroom and listened to Jessica throwing up. Travis debated whether or not to go in the bathroom and check on her. Finally, he decided to see if he could help her. He opened the door and knelt down next to Jessica. He held her hair back as she vomited. Travis rubbed her back in a comforting manor. He did not know what else to do for her. She finished and asked him to help her into the living room. Travis helped her sit down on the couch.

"Are you okay?" he asked.

"I'll live," she mumbled.

"Can I get you anything?"

"There is nothing you can get me. And there is nothing I can take," she answered him. She rubbed her forehead with a shaky hand.

Travis knelt down next to her on the floor. He stroked her hair. "You didn't have morning sickness with Abby."

She closed her eyes and willed her stomach to stop churning. "No two pregnancies are the same."

Travis continued to stroke her hair. "I wish there was something I could do to make you feel better. Are you sure you don't want something?"

Jessica jerked her head away from his touch. He was getting to close. "Get me some ginger ale," she ordered. She saw a flash of hurt in Travis's eyes.

"Sure, I'll get it for you," he said, getting up from the floor. He went into the kitchen and walked over to the refrigerator. He pulled out a can of ginger ale. Travis also grabbed a box of saltines off the cabinet. He walked back into the living room. "Here you go," he said, handing them to her. Travis took a blue afghan from the recliner and put it around her shoulders.

"Travis, you don't have to hover over me," she snapped. Jessica shrugged off the afghan and tossed it back on the chair. "I just want to be left alone."

Travis felt hurt. *I am just trying to make her feel better,* he thought to himself. "I guess I can't do anything right." He turned and stomped upstairs. He slammed the door to his room shut. *I was just trying to help her.*

Downstairs Jessica pounded the armrest of her chair with her fist. She sighed and got up. She knew that she should apologize to him. Jessica went up to the guest bedroom and knocked on the door. "Travis, can I come in?"

He opened the door, "What do you want?"

She looked at him and tried to give him a smile, but she could not quite do it. "I wanted to apologize to you. You have been really wonderful to me. You dropped everything to stay with me. I should act more grateful to you. I shouldn't have snapped at you. And for that I am sorry."

Travis shrugged his shoulders and turned around. He walked over to his desk and began to shuffle through the papers. "It's okay."

"Is that all you are going to say?" She wanted to know as she stepped into his room. "I said I was sorry."

Travis refused to look at her. "I know you are sorry." He held up some paper and waved them in her direction. "I need to go over this information."

Jessica knew him better than that. He was going to act like everything was fine when it was not. "Travis, don't be like this. I didn't mean to hurt your feelings." Jessica could feel tears building behind her eyes. "You have done so much for me, and I have been mean to you." She began to sob. "I don't know why I am acting like this."

Travis sighed and put the papers down. He went to her and pulled her into an embrace. Her body shook with sobs. "It's okay, Jessie. I should have been more understanding." He stroked her hair.

Jessica held on to him tightly. "I hate feeling like this." She wiped a glob of snot off her face.

"Like what?"

She buried her face in his chest. "That I need you. I feel so vulnerable and I hate it."

Travis pulled her away so she could look him in the eyes. "There is nothing wrong with that." He put the palms of his hands on her cheeks and wiped the tears off with his thumbs.

"It scares me."

Travis was about to ask her why when the phone rang. He dropped his hands and walked over to his nightstand and picked up the phone. "Hello, Moore residence."

"Hello, this is Dr. Morgan's office."

Travis looked over at the clock on the wall. They were an hour late for their appointment. "We missed the appointment. Can we still come in today?" he asked.

"Yes, we do have an opening in twenty minutes. Can you make it?" the woman wanted to know.

"We can," Travis said, and hung up the phone. He looked over at Jessica. "Come on. We are late for your ultrasound."

* * * * * * * * * * * *

Jessica was lying on the examination table as Dr. Morgan poured a cold jelly on her round stomach. She picked the paddle and smile down at her patient. "Are you ready?"

Jessica met her eyes. "I guess." She was scared stiff. She feared that the doctor would discover that there was something seriously wrong with her baby. She did not think she could survive such news. She held out her hand to Travis and he grasped it.

"Don't worry, Jessica, this won't hurt one bit," Dr. Morgan promised.

"I am not worried about me. I am worried about my baby." She felt tears come to her eyes again. "I am scared," she told them, looking from one to the other.

Travis bent over her and whispered in her ear, "It's going to be okay. Everything is fine."

You don't know that, Jessica thought to herself.

"Just relax, Jessica," Dr. Morgan ordered, as she ran the paddle over her stomach. She stared at the computer screen in front of her. She looked at it intensely. After a few minutes she smiled and turned the computer screen so Travis and Jessica could see it clearly. "Jessica, look."

Jessica looked at the monitor and smiled. She could see the baby floating around inside of her. She looked over at Travis and asked him, "Do you see our baby?"

"No," he admitted sadly.

"Here is the head." The doctor pointed it out with her pen. She then pointed out the arms and legs.

Travis now could see the baby. He was amazed at the image on the screen. "Is the baby alright?" He could not take his eyes off the screen.

"Everything looks good," she assured them. Jessica and Travis breathed a sigh of relief. "Let's listen to the heart." Dr. Morgan turned a knob on the machine and they could hear a loud thumping sound.

Jessica was alarmed over the fast sound. *There is something wrong with my baby after all,* she thought. Jessica's heart began to pound with fear. "There is a problem with the baby's heart, isn't there?"

"No, honey, that's normal." She turned off the machine and gave them both a smile. "I am pleased with everything I have seen today." She made some notes in the file. "Unless you have some problems, or questions, I'll see you in a few weeks."

* * * * * * * * * * *

Abby returned home from New York Sunday evening. She stepped into the house and smelled lasagna. The smell filled the whole house. Abby looked over at her father and gave him a smile. "You made lasagna?" she asked. The last time that she could remember him making it was when they lived in Montana.

Travis nodded. "I thought you deserved a nice home coming."

Abby gave him a hug. "Thanks. You know I love your lasagna," she patted her flat belly. "I'll probably have to go on a diet tomorrow though."

Travis laughed and went into the kitchen. Jessica reached over and tugged at her daughter's hand. "Sit down and tell me all about New York. I am sorry you didn't win the contest. But I am very proud of you."

Travis came out of the kitchen wiping his hands on a paper towel. "I am proud of you too, Abby." He tossed the towel into the trashcan. "Well, I'll go upstairs and pack."

"Your leaving?" Abby asked, disappointed that her scheme had failed. She had believed that having them spend time together would reunite them.

"Yeah, I have to go." He walked up stairs to get his suitcases.

Abby looked at her mother with disappointment in her eyes. "You and Dad aren't back together?"

Jessica smoothed Abby's hair out of her face. "No, we aren't, sweetie."

"Why not?"

"Well, I got everything and I am ready to go," Travis said, interrupting them. He tried to sound more upbeat than what he felt. He hated the thought of leaving Abby and Jessica.

Abby gave her mother a knowing look and then looked at Travis. Jessica knew that Abby wanted her to invite him to stay for dinner. She decided to give into her daughter's pressure. "Travis, please stay for dinner. You worked so hard on it. You should be able to enjoy it, too."

Travis shook his head. "I have a rally tonight that is crucial," he explained to them. He snapped his fingers. He had an idea. "Why don't the two of you come with me?" He looked at Jessica and then Abby. "And when it's done we can have dinner."

"No, I don't think so, Travis."

Travis nodded. He figured that Jessica would not agree to go to the rally. He turned his attention to Abby. "Will you walk me to my car?"

Abby got up from the couch and Jessica stopped her. "Abby, wait a minute. I need to speak with your father privately. Why don't you wait for him out by his car?" Jessica asked her.

Abby shrugged and walked out the door. Travis sat down on the couch where Abby had been sitting. "What is it, Jessica?"

She met his gaze. "I want to remember what you promised me. You won't use the children and me to gain votes. You'll keep us out of your campaign."

Travis held her gaze with his. "I promise, Jessica."

Jessica hoped that he was telling her the truth. She was trusting him. She hoped that she was not making a mistake. Jessica stood up and Travis did the same thing. "We better go outside. Abby will be waiting." They headed toward the door. Before he opened it she put a hand out to stop him. "One more thing. Thank you for staying with me."

"You don't have to thank me."

"Yes, I do. I was not the easiest person to get a long with these last couple of days." Jessica gave him a gentle hug.

"Your welcome," he said, breathing in her perfume. He wanted to savor this moment. He did not know when he would get to hold her again. Jessica pulled away from him and he opened the door. Abby was sitting on the trunk of his car waiting on him. She got off of it and he pushed the trunk button on his key chain. He put the suitcases in the trunk that Abby had brought out for him. He gave his daughter a bear hug. "I love you."

Abby hugged him back half-heartedly. *If he loves me so much then why can't we be a family again?* Abby thought sadly to herself. Then it came to her. He was ashamed of her. Despite what he had told her, he was ashamed of her. He

103

was more worried about his political career than her. It was her fault that her parents broke up. Abby let him go and headed back inside the house.

Travis watched her with growing unease. She was not acting like herself. He looked at Jessica. "I am worried about her."

"She'll be okay. She is just tired," Jessica said, trying to ease his worry. "I'll keep you posted on her."

Travis got into his car and drove off. Jessica turned and headed back into the house. She was just as worried about Abby as Travis was. Abby was sitting on the chair that was next to the window. He legs were pulled up to her chest and she was staring out the window. She watched her father drive off. She did not even look up when her mother touched her shoulder. "Abby?"

"Hmm?"

"Are you alright?"

"I am fine. I was just thinking," Abby said.

Jessica pulled her out of the chair. "Come on," she said. Her motherly intuition was telling her something was going on. Maybe, she could pry it out of her over dinner. She towed her into the kitchen. "You were going to tell me all about New York."

* * * * * * * * * * *

The next morning Brad was alone in Travis's hotel room. He had not been happy that Travis had arrived at the rally by himself. The guy was not doing anything to help his campaign. Brad sat down at the desk and began concentrating on a calendar. He was trying to figure out the best time for Travis to begin his bus tour. The phone next to his elbow rang. *Oh, now what?* he wondered. Brad sighed and sat back in the chair. He picked up the phone half expecting Abby or Jessica. "Hello?"

"Hello, is Senator Moore available?"

"No, he isn't it. May, I take a message?" he asked. Brad reached over and took a piece of hotel stationary and picked up a pen. He could not place the voice on the phone.

"This is Dr. Morgan's nurse. I just wanted to remind him of the appointment on Thursday at two o'clock."

Brad leaned forward on the desk. He clicked the pen. "I am not familiar with Dr. Morgan. Who is that?" he asked her. "I am Senator Moore's campaign manger. If he is ill I should know."

"Oh, no, nothing like that," she reassured him. "Dr. Morgan is an obstetrician. The senator's wife is pregnant."

Jessica is pregnant? Why didn't Travis tell me? We could use this to our advantage, he thought. "How far along is Mrs. Moore?"

"About five months," she told him. Brad could hear someone talking to her and after a minute she spoke to him again. "I have to go. Will you make sure that Senator Moore gets the message?"

"I will." He hung up the phone and sat back in his chair. *Well, well, well. This is an interesting turn of events,* Brad thought, forming a plan. They could use this information to their advantage. Travis had prevented him using the pictures of O'Neil and the hooker. But this was different. Brad picked up the phone and dialed a number. After telling his story he hung up. He sat back in his chair feeling very pleased with himself. He tapped his hands together and chuckled.

Travis came into his hotel room and saw Brad. "What are you doing here, Brad?" he asked, tossing his briefcase on the neatly made bed.

Brad sat up and held up a calendar. "Just trying to figure out a perfect time for you to go on your bus tour," he explained. "I want you to get a head start on O'Neil. So I think if you were to leave in two months it will give you a lead over him." He opened up a map of the United States and traced out a route with his finger. "You'll go through Indiana, Illinois, and finish in Minnesota."

"Sounds good," he said, looking at the map. Travis loosened his tie. "I'll go as long as Jessica…thinks Abby will be alright," he said quickly.

"Always thinking about your family. That's good."

"I would do anything for my family, Brad," Travis retorted.

Brad folded the map up. "Save it for the campaign trail, Travis. You are going to need it." He looked up and gave him a smile. "You should take Jessica and Abby with you on the bus tour. Americans have a soft spot for politicians with young families." He gave Travis a suggestive smile. "It could be a second honeymoon for you and Jessica."

Travis ignored the jibe. "I don't think they will want to go." In fact he knew that Jessica would not feel like going. And Abby would not want to be put on display. "And I am not going to force them to do something that they don't want to do."

Brad shrugged it did not matter. Not now anyway. "Well, I have some things I need to take care of. I'll see you later."

Travis waved at him as he went out the door. Travis worked until six and decided to call it a day. He took off his reading glasses and rubbed his eyes. He thought about calling Jessica, but he changed his mind. He decided to go to the house and visit them.

After a fifteen-minute drive he arrived at the house. He knocked on the door and Nancy answered. "Senator Moore!" she exclaimed.

"Hi, Nancy. Is my wife and daughter home?" he asked, stepping into the house.

"Yes sir, but I don't think they'll want to see you."

"Why not?" he asked in confusion.

"I'll tell you why," he heard an angry Jessica. She came to the door carrying a rolled up newspaper in her hand. She thrust it at him. "How could you, Travis? How could you break your promise to me? Just so you could win the election?"

Travis unrolled the newspaper and looked at the headline. He felt heart dropped to his feet. The headline read: 'Presidential candidate and wife to have a child'. "Oh, no," he whispered. He looked back at Jessica. "I didn't authorize this story, I swear."

"Don't lie to me. Who else could have done it? You are the only one who could have done it. No one else knows I am pregnant." Her green eyes filled with tears. She blinked them back. She refused to let him see her cry. "You promised that you would not use me or the children like this." She yanked the paper out of his hands. Jessica began to read from the paper. "My wife and I are expecting our second child and could not be happier. She and my daughter will be accompanying me on the bus tour," she stopped reading and glared at him. "How could give this story to the paper? Is the election so much more important than us?"

He tried to reach out to her, but she pushed him away. "Jessica, I did not do this. You have to believe me," he begged her.

"Was it worth it?" Jessica did not believe him. She could not believe that he had betrayed her like this. She wanted to hurt him for using her and the children like this. "Leave Travis. I can't stand the sight of you right now."

"Mom, who is at the door?" Abby asked, coming into the front hall. She scowled when she saw her father standing there. "What are you doing here?"

Jessica felt like the situation was spinning out of control. "Abby, go back to your room. I'll handle this."

"Mom…"

Travis broke in, "I will figure out who gave that story to the paper." He looked directly into Jessica's mad eyes. "Then I'll be back with proof that I didn't betray you." Travis took the paper out of Jessica's hands. He turned and walked out the door. Travis got back into his Mercedes and headed to the local park to think.

Once there he parked his car and got out. There were a few mothers with their young children. Two toddlers were being pushed on the swings while another one was sliding down the slide. He smiled wistful at them and sat down at a picnic table. He propped head on to his fist and stared off into the distance. He shook himself back into reality and unfolded the paper. In the story he supposedly claimed that Jessica was pregnant and that Abby had not been in a rehab clinic. That they were going to accompanying him on his bus tour. Travis waded the paper up and threw it in the trashcan. *No wonder Jessica and Abby were so mad. That story has things that Jessica and I would only know. Brad doesn't even know that Jessica…wait a minute Brad!* It hit him like a ton of bricks. Travis remembered seeing a message that Brad had taken from Dr. Morgan's office. It would not have been too hard for Brad to get information out of them. And he knew about Abby as well. He had been the one to suggest that they keep quite about Abby. Brad had warned him that Abby going to A.A meetings could get out to the press. *Brad did this,* he thought, getting up and jogging to his car. *He is going to pay for this,* Travis promised himself.

Travis drove downtown where Brad's office was. He went inside the office and barged into Brad's private office. "Travis, what are you doing here?" he asked. Travis could see that there was fear in his eyes.

Travis grabbed him by the shoulders and threw him into the wall. The pictures that were hanging on the wall fell to the floor in a loud crash. He knocked over the fern that was sitting in the corner. "You are the one who gave that story in 'The Voice,' didn't you?" Brad did not answer so Travis slammed him against the wall again. "Didn't you?"

"What's gotten into you, Travis?" he demanded, trying to break free of the hold.

"You are responsible for that story in the 'The Voice.' Now Jessica thinks I betrayed her. She hates me."

He continued to struggle. "She'll get over it. Give her some time," Brad told him. "Just think of what the story will do for your campaign."

"I don't care about my campaign. I care about my family." He slammed Brad into the wall for a third time.

"What is going on in here?" Brad's secretary asked. She gasped in horror when she saw that Travis had a hold of Senator Johnson. She ran out of the room. "Security! Security!" she yelled out.

Two burly men came running into the office and pulled Travis off of Brad. "Let him go," one of them ordered

Heather Dawn Thoroman

Travis. They held on to him so he could not attack Brad again.

He jerked out of the security men grasp. He straightened his jacket and adjusted his tie. "Your fired, Brad." He walked out of the office.

"You'll never win the presidency without me!" he heard Brad yell after him.

Travis did not answer Brad. If he had to resort to betraying the one's he loved most to win the election, he did not want to be president.

Travis had to tell Jessica that it had been Brad that had given out the story to 'The Voice' under his name. Some how he was going to make things right between them again. Before long he was ringing the doorbell to his house again. Jessica opened the door and sighed. "Travis…"

Travis stepped inside the house quickly and shut the door. "Jessica, listen to me. It was Brad who told, 'The Voice,' that you were pregnant not me. Brad was the one who said that you and Abby were going with me on the bus tour." He had to make her believe him.

Jessica was overwhelmed. She had some doubts about Travis's guilt after he left. Jessica wanted to believe that, but it was hard. "I want to believe you."

"Jessica, I would never betray you like that. You know that I wouldn't."

Jessica looked into his blue eyes. There was only honesty in them. What he was saying did have a ring of truth to it. She knew that Travis would respect her and Abby's privacy. Brad on the other hand was ruthless and would do anything to get Travis to win the election. "I believe you," she admitted. "I should have believed you from the beginning."

Travis felt relief wash over him. She believed him. He wanted to take her in his arms, but the look on her face stopped him. He realized that she was still worried about Brad. "You don't have to worry about Brad anymore, Jess. I fired him."

"It's not Brad that I was thinking about," she told him. Jessica walked over to the picture window. She kept her back to him so he would not see that her eyes were filled with tears. *This is so hard,* Jessica thought to herself. "Travis, I have been thinking about moving back to Montana."

Travis walked over to her. His eyes narrowed as he asked, "What did you say?"

"I have been thinking about moving back to Montana," she repeated.

Travis took her shoulder and turned her around so she would face him. "Jessica, why would you want to move? I am here. Our life is here. Not in Montana."

"I don't want to move, Travis. But I have to do what is best for my children." She picked up the newspaper and waved it in his direction. "Do you want to know what this story did to Abby?"

"What?" he asked in alarm.

"She was upset. She thought it was true. She told me that she did not want to travel around for two months in a R.V. while people asked her personal questions and took pictures. She begged me not to go. It took me a long time to convince her that she did not have to go."

Travis looked toward the stairs and then back at Jessica. Concern was written on his face. "Where is she know?" he asked, remembering that she had been upset earlier when he was there. "I want to see her."

Jessica pushed past him. "She is at an A.A. meeting."

"Oh."

Jessica sat down on the chair. She put her hands on her stomach. Jessica rubbed her tummy and mentally told her baby that everything was going to be okay. She then turned her attention back to her husband. "Travis, this is hard for me. I have to protect my children anyway I can. And moving back to Montana is the best way to do that. I have to get them away from this city. Get them away from all this pressure."

He gave her a furious look. Travis stood in front of her with his arms folded. "I won't let you take my children away from me. I'll fight you with everything I got," he threatened.

"Travis, don't be like this," she begged. Her vision became bleary. *Can't he see that this is the best thing for Abby?* she asked herself.

"You are making me do this. You are the one who wants to move my children across the country. You are the one trying to shove me out of my children's lives."

Jessica got up. She made him look her in the eye. She could see the intense hurt and vulnerability in them. Jessica hated hurting him like this. "I am not trying to push you out of the children's lives. I would never do that to you. But if you thought about it, you would realize that this is the best thing for them," she tried to reason with him. "I want to protect them."

He yanked his hands away from hers. Travis backed away. "You want to protect them from me. This is the best thing for you. You never liked living here. You never liked me being in politics."

Now she was as mad at him as he was at her. "You're right. I hate the fact that you are in politics. I hate always being on display. I hate this fishbowl that we have been living in for the last few years. I hate the pressure. I have to get out of here."

Travis jaw tightened and he turned away from her. "I am losing my family," he said softly. Travis looked up to the ceiling and blinked back tears. He closed his eyes tightly so he would not cry.

Jessica put a hand on his back. "Travis?"

Travis faced her. Jessica sucked in a deep breath. She was scared over how he was looking at her. There was a hard dead look in his gaze. "I am not going to let you take my children away from me." He walked past her.

Travis headed for the front door. Suddenly, he felt a sharp pain shoot through his chest. The pain left him gasping for breath. The pain was getting worse and was now radiating down his left arm. Travis reached out and grabbed doorway. He fell to one knee.

"Travis!" Jessica cried out in fear. She reached his side as fell all the way to the floor. "Travis!"

He was breathing hard. He could not catch his breath at all. Travis looked at Jessica's face. He could see terror on her face. Darkness was closing in on him. If he was going to die, the last face he wanted to see was Jessica's.

Chapter Ten

Jessica was sitting in an orange plastic chair in the Emergency Room waiting area. She ignored the elderly man who was sitting on the couch on the other side of the waiting room. He had a heart broken expression on his face. Any other time she would have comforted him, but now she was to absorbed in her own fears. Jessica was desperate for news about Travis. She was scared to death that Travis was going to die. Plus, she was overwhelmed with guilt. If they had not been fighting he would be all right. She wrapped her arms around her budding stomach and pleaded with God to save her husband's life.

"Mom!" Abby cried out, as she came running into the Emergency room. "What happened? Is dad okay?"

Jessica pulled her daughter into her a hug. Jessica was relived that Abby was there. She stroked Abby's hair. She had left a note at home for Abby to get to the hospital as soon as possible. "Dad collapsed in the front hall." She left out the part where they had been in a shouting match when he collapsed. She pulled away from Abby. Jessica put her hands on each side of Abby's face and made her look at her. "Daddy's going to fine. He is strong. He is not going to let this keep him down for long."

"He'll be fine," Abby repeated, trying to convince herself. As mad as she was at her father, she did not want him to die. "He has to be." Jessica gave her another comforting hug. Abby burst into tears and laid her head on Jessica's shoulder. Jessica cried right along with her.

The door to the Emergency room opened and Dr. Martin came out followed by another doctor. "Mrs. Moore?" he called out.

Jessica let go of Abby. She took her hand and went over to the doctors stood. "I am Travis Moore's wife," *He must not remember me,* Jessica thought absent-mindedly.

Dr. Martin shook hands with both Abby and Jessica and indicated to his colleague. "This is Dr. Hendrickson. He is our best cardiologist. He'll be able to give a better prospective on how your husband is doing."

Dr. Hendrickson was a short, plump, bald headed man. He gave them a tired smile and shook hands with them as well. "Let's sit down." He helped Jessica into a chair. "I wish I could give you better news, but I am afraid I can't. Senator Moore has a had a heart attack."

Both Jessica and Abby sucked in breaths. "Was it a serious one?" Jessica wanted to know.

"It was bad enough," he admitted to them. "It was not a serious attack, but bad enough that I am concerned."

"Will he die?" Abby cried out.

Dr. Hendrickson handed Abby some Kleenex and patted her on the shoulder in a fatherly way. "Your father will have to be closely monitored for the next couple of days. If everything looks good, I'll send him home," he then turned serious. "But he will have to make some life style changes. He'll have to change his diet and go on an exercise program. And he will have to reduce his stress level."

Jessica nodded in agreement. She was relieved that Travis's condition was not too serious. But she was still concerned about him. She knew that Travis would continue to work at the same level as he always did. Despite what the doctors told him. *If we had not been arguing maybe he would be all right,* she thought. "Can we see him?" she asked the cardiologist.

"You can visit him for five minutes. He is still very weak. And he needs his rest," the doctor said and stood up. He led them to Travis's room in the cardiology intensive care unit. The unit was in a shape of a horseshoe with six cubicles in all. The nurse's desk was in the center so they could monitor the patients easily. "Five minutes," he reminded them as they entered the room.

Jessica was not listening to him. She went to her husband's bedside. She was devastated when she got a good look at him. Travis looked awful. His skin was ashen and he looked twice his age. Travis had an oxygen tube in his nose and I.V lines coming out of his arms. The heart monitor let out a reassuring beep. Jessica took his hand and was dismayed at how frail if felt to her. She leaned over and stroked his hair. "It's okay, Travis. Abby and I are here." She reached over and pulled Abby closer to the bed.

Abby did not want to get closer to the bed. She was terrified over how her father looked. *He doesn't even look like he is alive,* Abby thought horrified. Her mother gave her hand a comforting squeeze. "Hi, Daddy," she said, hoping that maybe her father would hear her and wake up.

Travis's eyes opened. They fluttered shut and then they opened again. He looked over at Jessica and Abby. "Hi, girls," he said weakly.

Jessica swallowed back her tears. She had to be strong for both Travis and Abby. His eyes looked vacant and his hand was cold. "How do you feel?" she asked feeling stupid. She already knew how he felt. Awful.

"I am sorry," his voice was nothing more than a whisper. "I am sorry for everything."

Jessica leaned to him. "Don't worry about that now, Travis. Just focus on getting better," she said in his ear. "Abby and I want you to get well fast so you come home." Jessica put his limp hand on her stomach. "You need to get better. We need you."

Travis's eyes closed again. He gave her a faint smile. "I feel the baby." His breathing became deeper as he slipped into a drug-induced sleep.   Jessica laid his hand back on the bed gently so not to wake him. She had been surprised when he said he felt the baby move. She had not felt anything. But if that is what he thought, then that she would let him believe it.

"Mom?" Abby asked, taking a step closer to her.

"We should go and let your father rest," Jessica nodded toward the door. They left the room and went into the waiting room. Jessica collapsed into a chair and burst into tears. Everything that she had been holding in came out. "He looks so bad." she wept.

Abby felt her own tears come to her eyes. But she was going to strong for her mother. "Like you said earlier he is strong. He's a survivor."

Jessica nodded her head. She blew her nose on a tissue and turned to Abby. "He's a survivor," she repeated. She looked toward Travis's hospital room and fell apart again.

* * * * * * * * * * * *

The next morning Jessica entered Travis's room and was happy to discover him sitting up in bed. He looked better than he had the night before. Travis was still pale and he looked weak, but he did look better. He gave her a smile when he saw her standing there. "Hi, Jess," his voice sounded raspy.

Jessica sat down next to his bed. "How do you feel?"

Travis sat up more in bed. "Better. But I still feel like I have been run over by a semi." He met her eyes and she could see a little twinkle in them. "I hope someone got the license plate number."

Jessica could not help but giggle. She knew he was trying to put her at ease. "Don't worry they'll catch it."

Travis chuckled and then stopped. He laid back against the pillows and closed his eyes. He took several deep breaths. His face got a little paler. When he reopened his eyes, Travis saw Jessica standing over him. There was concern written on her face. He took her hand. "I am fine," he assured her.

"Are you sure? I can get a nurse."

"No."

Jessica was about to argue when Dr. Hendrickson came in. He nodded at Jessica and gave her a smile. He stepped over to Travis's bed. "How are you doing, Senator Moore?"

"I have been better."

Dr. Hendrickson took the stethoscope from around his neck and put the earpieces in his ears. He listened to Travis's heart for a few minutes. He then put the stethoscope back around his neck. He made a few notes in his chart.

"How's my husband?" Jessica demanded.

Dr. Hendrickson finished making his notes and looked at Jessica and Travis. "Everything sounds good. I am going to schedule the senator for a echocardiogram for later this afternoon." He closed the chart and put it under his arm. "If everything looks good, I'll release him on Wednesday."

"Good," Travis said, "I have work that I need to do."

Jessica felt a sting of fear go through her. She was scared that he was going to work himself to death. "Dr. Hendrickson, would you please tell him that he is going to have to slow down." She gave Travis a frustrated look. *You would think that this heart attack would be warning enough for him,* she thought, feeling her frustration grow.

"Your wife is right, Senator Moore," his doctor agreed. "You are going to have to make some changes in your life. You are going to have to reduce your stress level. You can't keep working like you have been." He gave Travis serious look. "This heart attack was just a warning. The next time you might not be so lucky."

"He'll do what ever you suggest," Jessica told him. She glared at Travis as if she were daring him to cross her. "I'll make sure of that."

"Good. I'll check on you later." Dr. Hendrickson walked out of the room.

Travis looked over at Jessica. "Thank you for staying with me." He took her hand. "I don't want to be alone right now," he confessed.

Jessica gently squeezed his hand. "You won't be alone. I am going to be right here," she promised. She stroked his gray hair with her free hand.

Travis closed his eyes and for a minute she thought that he had fallen asleep, but he reopened his eyes. "You were right. I have been so obsessed with my own career that I have ignored my family." He gave her a sad smile. "I don't want to die with my family in pieces."

Jessica went cold with fear. She could not bear the thought of losing him. "Travis, you are not going to die," she exhaled noisily. "I want our family back together, too." She saw the hopeful look in Travis's eyes and continued on. "But I don't know how to do it. We want two different things for our family."

Travis let go of her hand and let out a shaky breath. He did not know how to repair their family. He wanted his family and his career. But he did not know how he could keep both. Suddenly, he was exhausted. "I am tired. I think I am going to take a nap." He rolled over and faced the wall. Tears slipped down his cheeks. He made sure that Jessica did not see them.

Jessica touched his back tenderly. "I'll let you get some rest. I'll be back later." She got up from her chair and headed out the door.

Travis rolled over and watched as Jessica walked out of his room. "What am I going to do?" he asked himself.

* * * * * * * * * * * *

Abby walked into the First Assembly of God Church basement where the A.A. meetings were held. So far she was the only one there. Abby knew that it would be filling up quickly in the next thirty minutes. She saw her sponsor Melissa Connor setting up the chairs for the meeting. Abby walked over to her. "Hi, Melissa. Can I help?"

Melissa pushed her blond hair our of her eye and gave Abby a grateful smile. "Thank you. I don't know where Mark is. He was supposed to be helping me," she unfolded the chair. "How are you doing, Abby?" she asked.

Abby took one of the chairs and unfolded. She placed it next to the one Melissa had set up. "Not to good," she admitted to her sponsor. "Dad had a heart attack yesterday."

Melissa stopped what she doing and looked at Abby with concern. She reached over and took one of Abby's hands. "I am sorry. How is doing?"

"He is doing better. He should be getting out of the hospital in a couple of days."

"That's good," she continued to a stare at Abby. She could tell Abby was upset. "Tell your father that I hope he feels better soon."

Abby nodded, but she had other things on her mind. In fact she was feeling desperate. "Melissa, can we talk before the meeting?"

Melissa had been involved with Alcoholic Anonymous long enough to know when someone was in trouble. She slipped easily into the role of councilor. "Sure we can," she pointed to the chair and they sat down. "What's going on?"

"I know why my dad moved out. It was not to protect me from the media. It was to protect him," Abby told her. "He is ashamed of me."

Melissa put her elbows on her knees and leaned forward. She kept her head turned in Abby's direction. "I don't believe that."

"It's true, Melissa! He never visited me while I was at rehab. He never wrote and he never called me. Not once the whole time I was there! Dad did not want it getting out that I was there. He had to protect his image." Abby got up from the chair and started pacing back and forth. "He is more concerned about his career than me. It does not look good when a presidential candidates daughter is a drunk." She pointed a finger in Melissa's direction. "Did you know it was my mom who got me into rehab? Dad did not even want me to go."

Melissa watched Abby as she had her tirade. She was making her nervous with her angry pacing. "Abby, I know that you are hurt and angry at your father right now. But it is difficult for him to realize that you have a problem. A lot parents don't want to face the truth for one reason or another."

"Like they are ashamed of them."

"No, because they are afraid. They are scared that they are going to lose their child," Melissa said. She paused and looked down at her hands. "My younger sister Jami was an alcoholic. My father kept saying that she was just experimenting. 'It's just phase', he would tell my mother. Well, she experimented herself right into a grave at sixteen." She looked up at Abby with tears in her eyes. "That is why I got involved with troubled kids. I did not want another family to suffer like mine did."

Abby sat down next to Melissa in shock. She had never heard that story before. "Wow Melissa," she was unsure of what else to say. "I am sorry about your sister. That's rough."

Melissa gave her a sad smile. "You remind me so much of Jami. I think that is why we got a long so good from the beginning." She reached over and pulled Abby into a hug. "I want to see you succeed in your recovery. And I know your parents do, too." She let go of her. "Despite, what you think, I know that your father is proud of you. He is not ashamed of you. In fact, he might be ashamed of himself."

Abby did not believe Melissa about her father. Melissa did not see that look in his eyes like she had. Travis was ashamed of her. He could not stand having her as a daughter.

* * * * * * * * * * * *

Wednesday Travis was released from the hospital. Jessica had insisted that he stay with her and Abby for a few days. When they arrived at the house Travis got out of the car and took a deep breath, "Hmm. Freedom." He could still smell the hospital on his clothes.

Jessica giggled and took his arm and they walked to the house. "You have to rest a week before you go back to work. And when you do go back to work it will be at a reduced schedule," she reminded him, as she opened the door. Jessica called out for their daughter, "Abby, we are home! Come and see your father!"

Abby came out of the kitchen. She looked at her father without even smiling. "Hi," she mumbled. Abby made no move to go to him.

Travis walked over to Abby and gave her a hug. "Hi honey. I have missed you."

Abby shrugged out of his grasp. She did not care what Melissa had told her. She still believed that Travis was ashamed of her. And she also believed she had been abandoned by him, too. "I have homework I need to do." She turned on her heel and went back into the kitchen. *If he can ignore me, I can ignore him, too,* she thought seething.

Travis took a step toward the kitchen, but Jessica stopped him from going in. "I'll talk to her later. But for now lets give her some space," she told him. She led him to the couch and told him to sit down.

"I am worried about her, Jessica. I don't want her to start drinking again."

Jessica was about to reply when she felt a gentle movement in her stomach. "Oh!" she cried out in surprise. She put both hands on her stomach.

Travis looked at her in alarm. He was switching to crisis mode. "What's wrong?" He felt his heart rate go up. *There is something wrong with the baby,* Travis thought in a panic. He started to get up.

Jessica reached over and stopped him. She put his hand on her stomach. Her skin felt soft and warm to the touch. He looked at her curious as to what she was up to. After a few seconds he felt a gentle movement. He looked up at her beaming face. "The baby moved," he said happily.

"It's amazing isn't it?" She continued to feel her baby moving around. Travis kept his hand on her stomach. "It's a miracle."

Travis reached over with his free hand and touched her cheek. "Thank you for making me a father again."

Jessica met his happy gaze with her own. "Thank you for making me a mommy again," she said. Travis leaned forward and gave her a sweet kiss on the lips. She kissed him back. She was willing to pretend that things were fine between them for a little while. They sat on the couch for the rest of the afternoon feeling their baby move.

* * * * * * * * * * * *

The next day Travis was reading the newspaper when the doorbell rang. He checked his watch. She was right on time. He started to stand up when Jessica came out of the kitchen. "Don't get up," she told him. "I'll get it." She walked over to the door and opened it. She came to face to face with a dark haired woman. She was wearing a navy pinstriped suite and was carrying a briefcase in her right hand. She had an air of impatience about her. "Hello, may I help you?" Jessica asked her.

The woman pushed up her horn-rimmed glasses and nodded her head. "I am looking for Senator Moore. He is here?"

"Yes," Jessica admitted apprehensively. "Who are you? Why are you looking for my husband?"

"I am May Combs. I am his new campaign manager."

"Come on in, May," Jessica heard Travis say from behind her. "I am glad you made it. We have a lot of things to discuss." He shook May's hand. "We can work in my study." He led her toward his study.

Jessica grabbed him by his arm. "Wait a minute, Travis."

"Go through that door," Travis pointed toward his study. "I'll be there in a minute." He looked at Jessica in confusion. "What's going on?"

Jessica fixed him with an angry look. "Dr. Hendrickson told you that you had to rest. You shouldn't be working so soon after your heart attack."

Travis patted her hand. "I feel fine. Besides, we are not going to do a whole lot. I am just going to tell her what I have with my campaign so far," he gave her a patronizing smile. "I'll rest after May leaves."

Jessica jerked her hand away. She was not going to let him talk to her like she was a child. "If you don't care about your health, than neither do I. Just go ahead and work yourself to death." She stormed upstairs and slammed her bedroom door shut. *He doesn't care about me and the children. If he did he would be taking better care of himself,* she thought absent-mindedly, as picked up a sack of baby clothes from the floor. She sat down on her bed and began to fold them. *I want this baby to know its father. Is that too much to ask?*

Abby stuck her head into her mother's bedroom. "What's going on Mom? I thought I heard you yelling a minute ago."

Jessica beckoned for her to come into the room. "Yeah, your father is working, when the doctor specifically told him to rest." She handed Abby some blankets. "Fold these for me." Jessica blinked back tears of frustration. "That damn election."

Abby folded the multi colored receiving blankets and put them in a pile on the bed. "I guess it is just more important than us."

Jessica stopped folding the clothes and stared at her daughter in shock. *Where would she get an idea like that? Did she get that idea from me? I hope not,* she wondered. "Your father loves you."

"Right."

"Abby, listen to me. Yes, the election is important to him, but not more important than you. You are his top priority," Jessica said. *Who am I trying to convince? Her or me?* She had to ask herself. Jessica could tell that Abby did not believe her.

Abby rolled her eyes. "Yeah, I am very important to him. That is why he goes with me to the A.A meetings. That is why he went with you to all those Parents with Alcoholic Children meetings. He did not want anyone seeing him come out of those meetings. He could not risk it getting out that I have been going to those meetings. It could damage his public image." She folded her arms across her chest as if she were daring her mother to argue with her. "Dad's ashamed of me. And don't deny it."

Jessica opened and closed her mouth. She could not think of anything to say. She had been thinking the same thing for weeks, but had not said anything. She watched as

Abby stalked out of the bedroom. Jessica threw the tiny shirt down on the bed. She got up and headed back down stairs. Travis was going to talk to her now. Kay or May or whatever her name was could wait.

They were coming out of Travis's study as she was coming down the stairs. "Thanks for all the help, May. I think this is going to work out. You had some good ideas," Jessica heard him say. May nodded and went out the door. Travis turned around and saw her. "We are done and I am going to go upstairs and take a nap. Happy?"

"No, because we have another problem."

He looked at her with concern. "What is it?"

"It's Abby. She thinks that you are ashamed of her."

"What?" he asked stunned. "Where did she get an idea like that from?" Travis looked at Jessica with suspicion. "Do you tell her that?"

"No!" She gave him a disgusted look. "She just said it to me a minute ago. But I think she is right. You never came with me to any of the Parents with Alcoholic Children meetings. You never contacted her while she was in rehab." She hated to ask him, but she had to know the truth. "Are you ashamed of Abby?"

It was Travis's turn to look disgusted. "I am very proud of my daughter, Jessica."

"You did not answer my question, Travis. Are you embarrassed by her?" she pressed him.

Travis looked at the floor. He could not answer her. Maybe she embarrassed him. Just a little bit. But he was not going to let Jessica know that. He met her eyes, "I am not embarrassed by her and to prove it to both of you, I am taking you and Abby to the rally tomorrow night. I want to show both of you that I am proud of her."

Jessica sighed. She did not really want to go to the rally, but it sounded like she did not have much say in the decision. "Okay, we'll go. I hope we are not making a mistake."

<u>Chapter Eleven</u>

The loud pounding music made Jessica's headache worse. She put her fingers in her ears trying to drown out the pounding drums. It did not help. She watched as people ran around trying to figure out what was going to happen next. They yelled at one another to be heard over the music. But what they said was in contradiction to one another. Police were stationed at various places throughout the auditorium. They were ready for any trouble if it should arise. Travis and May were huddled together making last minute changes to his speech. And who knew where Abby was.

Jessica sighed. She wished she had not come. She had been feeling dizzy and nauseous most of the day. But if she had not gone to the rally, Travis would have accused her of turning Abby against him. She sat down on a metal folding chair. Jessica put a hand on her stomach.

"Mom!" Abby yelled. Jessica had not seen her come up. Abby dropped down to one knee next to the chair. She leaned closer to her mother's ear so she could hear her better. "Mom!"

Jessica looked at Abby. "What is it?"

Abby gave her a worried look. "You don't look like you feel good. Are you alright?"

Jessica was about to tell her she was fine when she felt a pain go through her abdomen. She clutched her stomach both hands. *No, please no,* she thought in fear. The cramp eased. Jessica took in a deep breath and let it out slowly. As the pain was easing another one hit. She doubled over in her chair.

"Mom!"

"Get your father! Hurry!" Jessica watched as Abby ran off to find Travis. She looked over to where Travis had been a second ago, but now he was gone. Jessica had not seen where he had gone. She hoped that Abby could find him. Jessica could hear Steve Blackwell's voice over the P.A. system.

"Now ladies and gentlemen, may I present to you the next President of the United States of America, Senator Travis Moore!" Steve announced, to the cheering crowd. The band began to play, *Hail to the Chief.* Jessica could hear the crowds cheering get louder. She knew that Travis had stepped out on to the stage.

Abby hurried back to her mother's side. "I couldn't find him." Her mother looked like she was about to pass out from the pain. She had to do something to help her. Abby looked over at the policemen standing by the door. She beckoned for one of them to come over to them. "Is there an ambulance outside?" she asked, as the officer jogged over.

"Yes, there is." He looked over at Jessica. "I'll have them pull up to the back door." He pulled out his walkie-talkie and began speaking into it.

Abby turned her attention back to Jessica. "It's going to be okay, Mom. Just stay calm. Why didn't you tell me you were feeling badly?"

Jessica shrugged her shoulders. She had not told Abby that this had been set up for her. To show her that Travis was not ashamed of her. Plus, if she had missed the rally he would have accused her of trying to turn Abby against him. She felt her contractions intensify. *If I lose my baby it's going to be my entire fault,* she thought despondently.

* * * * * * * * * * *

At the hospital Dr. Morgan leaned over Jessica and listened to the baby's heart. Once they had stabilized her, the contractions had stopped. She was still scared though. Jessica clutched the sheets in her hand as she watched the doctor listen to the heartbeat and removed her stethoscope. "Well?" she demanded, "is my baby okay?"

Dr. Morgan gave her a comforting smile and patted her hand. "Everything sounds good. Your contractions have stopped. But you need to relax, Jessica. Your blood pressure is elevated and that is not good for you or the baby," she explained. "That is why you felt poorly. I am going to get admitted." She made some notes in the chart. "I'll check on you later." She walked out of the cubicle.

As Doctor Morgan left, Travis rushed in. He picked up her hand. "How are you feeling? What did Dr. Morgan say?"

"She said my blood pressure was elevated. I need to relax so it will go back down."

"But you are okay? The baby is alright?"

"Yes. The contractions have stopped. Thank God," she said simply. Jessica pulled her hand away from his touch.

"I really thought I was losing the baby." She put her hands on her swollen stomach. "I want this baby more than anything."

Travis looked into her eyes. "Why didn't you tell me you were having pains? I would have come with you to the hospital." He had been terrified when he finished with his speech and Steve had told him that Jessica had been sent to the hospital. Travis had rushed to her side as soon as he had been told.

Jessica blinked back tears. "Travis, I did not want to disturb you. You were about to give your speech. I know how important this rally was to you."

"Not as important as you and baby are," he argued. Travis could see disbelief in her eyes. He realized that Jessica had been right along. The stress of the campaign was too much for and Abby to deal with. He had to do something that he did not want to do. But it was the best thing for Jessica and the children. "Maybe I should move back to the hotel. It would be best for both you and Abby."

Jessica did not say anything. She felt like he was abandoning her. *He is moving back into the hotel so he can work on the election undisturbed,* Jessica thought sadly. She refused to look him in the eye.

He leaned closer and tried to convince her that he had her best interest at heart. "I have seen first hand what the stress has done to you. I am not going to risk your health or the life of our baby," Travis realized that she did not believe him. He got up from the chair and hurried out of the room.

Jessica watched him go. *He says that your family is important to him, but actions speak louder than words,* she thought. *If he would work on our family as much as the election we would still be together.* She covered her eyes with her hands and began to cry.

* * * * * * * * * * * *

Now seven months pregnant, Jessica paced the floor in her living room while holding a cordless phone in her right hand. "Hello? Finally, I have been on hold for five minutes!"

"I am sorry, ma'am. How can Baby World help you today?" the male voice on the other end asked her.

"Somebody from your business was suppose to come at ten this morning to put together a crib for me. But no one ever showed up," she told him.

"I am sorry, ma'am. We are behind schedule. I was just getting ready to call you, Mrs. Moore. We won't be able to come over until Thursday of this week. Is that okay with you?"

"I guess it will have to be." She disconnected the phone and put it back in its cradle. She burst into tears.

"Mom, what's wrong? Is it dad? Did he have another heart attack? Is it the baby?" Abby asked in alarm, when she came into the living room and found her mother in tears.

"No, no, no," she assured Abby, as Jessica wiped her eyes. "It's just that..." she started sobbing harder.

Abby sighed. She walked over to Jessica and gave her a hug. *Hormones,* she thought. She helped her mom sit down on the couch and gave her some tissues. "Mom, you need to calm down. This is not good for you or the baby."

Jessica took a deep breath in hoping it would calm her down. She blew her nose. "I am sorry, Abby. I know that I am acting silly."

"It's alright, Mom."

Jessica felt her eyes fill up with tears again. *No, it's not all right,* she thought, looking at her daughter. "Your father is leaving tomorrow for his bus tour," Jessica told her, as she wiped the tears off her face. "I don't want him to go. What if he gets sick again?"

Abby felt a stab of fear shoot through her. That had been one of her biggest fears as well. But she could not let her mother know that. It would only upset her even more. "Mom, he is going to be fine. The doctor would not let him go if he thought dad was not well enough."

"I am going to have the baby while he is gone. I can't do this without him, Abby," Jessica added rubbing her stomach.

"You have another month and a half before the baby is born."

Jessica looked at her with wet eyes. "He'll be gone for the next two months. I am going to be alone when the baby comes."

Abby was stunned that her father would not be there for the baby's birth. She took a deep breath and tried to keep her temper. Now Abby knew why her mother was so upset. Abby knew that her mother was scared and needed someone to support her. And that someone was going to have to be Abby. She gave her mother's hand a squeeze. "Mom, you have me. I am going to be here with you. You'll be fine. Whatever comes up we'll deal with it."

Jessica let herself relax. She did feel better knowing that Abby would be with her. She pulled Abby into her arms and gave her a hug. "Thank you." She gave her a kiss on her cheek and pulled away. She gave her daughter a wobbly smile. "Your mother is silly, isn't she?"

Abby returned the smile. She felt pleased with herself. She had calmed her mother down. And she had convinced

Jessica that everything would be fine while her father was gone. *I hope I am right,* Abby thought to herself. *We can do this,* she thought, trying to bolster her confidence. There was a knock at the door and Abby sighed. She got up and went to the door. "Dad," she said, when she saw who it was.

"Hi, Abby," he leaned over and gave her a kiss on the cheek. "Is your mother here?"

"Where else would she be?" she asked, rolling her eyes. Abby was mad that he was leaving her mother. She had never so furious at her father. Her mother needed him more than any old dumb election did. But did he care? No. She stormed up the stairs so she would not have to deal with him. Abby did not care if she hurt his feelings.

Travis's eyes were filled with pain as he watched her go upstairs. She was even more hostile to him than usual. He sighed and turned to Jessica. "Hi, Jess, are you ready to go the Lamaze class?"

She folded her arms across her huge chest and glared at him. "Why bother? You won't be here for me when I do have the baby. So why are you going?" she demanded.

Travis sighed, "We have talked about this, Jessica. When you go into labor you have Abby call me and I'll get home as soon as I can."

"You won't get here in time. By the time you arrive the baby will have been born."

"You don't know that," he fought back. Travis forced her to look at him. "I am going to be here for you and the baby. I promise you that."

Jessica's eyes were still hard. She jerked away from him. "Don't make promises that you can't keep," she told him. Jessica grabbed her purse from the couch. She went upstairs to tell Abby that she was leaving. Jessica then came back down stairs.

"Jessica..." he said.

Jessica ignored him. She went out the door and walked out to her Cadillac. Travis had no choice but to follow her in his car. He hoped that she would eventually calm down and they could talk about this rationally. He was not abandoning her and Abby like they thought. He would never do that to them. He loved them too much to do something like that.

They arrived at the Y.M.C.A, where the Lamaze class was being held. Jessica got out of the car and hurried into the building. Travis walked after her. He was still determined to make her listen to him. They entered the building and Jessica went over to Holly, another mother-to-be. "Travis doesn't understand," he heard his wife tell Holly as he approached them.

"You need to make him understand your fears," Holly told her. She rubbed her own round belly.

"I have tried," Jessica said. Travis was right behind her. He touched her shoulder and she turned around. Travis could see tears in her eyes. He pulled her into his arms and held her close. Jessica laid her head on his chest. She cried tears of fear. "Why can't you understand that I need you here? Why can't you understand that I am scared?" she wept.

Travis stroked her hair in a comforting manner. He did understand what she was going through. *Would it be so bad to postpone the bus tour until the baby is born?* he asked himself. He did not say anything. He was torn over what he wanted to do. He did want to be there for his wife and the baby, but he was also worried about his campaign. Jessica seemed to sense that he was conflicted and pulled away and walked away from him. Travis watched her as she walked away.

An hour later the class was over and they were walking back to their cars. They had not said one word to one another. There was nothing to say to each other. Both felt hurt and confused. Jessica was about to get into the Cadillac, when suddenly there was a loud screeching sound. She looked up and saw an out of control car. A red sports car sped around a sharp corner and crossed the double line. The car ran off the road and slammed into a tree. The sound was deafening. "No!" Jessica cried out in horror.

Jessica pulled her cell phone out of her purse and dialed 911. "I want to report a car accident. On McKinnon Drive in front of the Y.M.C.A. A red car lost control and slammed into a tree." She looked over at Travis. "Go and check on the people in the car," Jessica ordered Travis. He did not answer her. His eyes were unfocused and it looked like he was in shock. "Travis?"

He blinked his eyes. Jessica could see the look of terror on his face. Travis looked at the car and backed away slowly at first. He then ran away. Jessica watched him stunned. She could not believe that he would runaway when there were people who needed his help. She walked over to the embankment and looked up at the other people who had stopped to see if they could help. "Are they alive?"

An older man looked down at her and shook his head. "No, he's dead. He must have been drunk. There are beer cans all over the floor of the car."

Jessica relayed the news to the dispatcher and closed her phone. She threw it in the car and went in the direction that Travis had gone. "Travis! Travis!" she screamed. She was not sure where he had gone. "Travis, where are you?"

Jessica heard him before she saw him. Travis was leaning against the side of the building. His hands covered his face and he cried great gulping sobs. She walked over to him and touched his shoulder. "Travis, what's wrong?"

Travis did not look at her. But he did drop his hands. "My brother," he mumbled. "My brother is dead."

"What are you talking about?" she asked. Jessica was scared. She had never seen him like this before. "Travis, what is going on with you?"

He looked at her with pain filled eyes. His breathing was hard and it sounded like he was not able to catch it. She was worried that he was having another heart attack. "My brother was killed in a car wreck."

Jessica was taken aback. "Your brother? You don't have a brother."

Travis did not answer her. He looked straight ahead and never met her gaze. "He was two years older than me." He looked over at her and gave her a slight smile. "He was my hero." The smile fell from his face and he got that far away look on his face again. "The night of his graduation we were at the Sundown Bar and Grill with a group of friends. We had been drinking for about an hour when we decided to go to the lake. I was going to take my car and Jake was going to go with his girlfriend. My girlfriend left her purse in the bar, so I went back to get it. The next thing I hear is this hideous crashing sound. I ran out and..." he stopped and buried his face in his hands. "Why did this have to happen? Why?" he cried.

Jessica put her arms around him. She was in shock. Travis had never told her the story before. She recalled a night several months ago when she had found him in the bathroom after a nightmare. *It was a repressed memory. No wonder he has had a hard time with Abby's alcoholism. I wish I had been more understanding.* "Travis, it's okay."

"The car blew up. My parents were devastated. They never forgave me for it," Travis let out a disgusting cough and bent over. Jessica rubbed his back as he vomited. When he finished he continued with his story. "Jake was their favorite son. He could do no wrong in our parent's eyes. I was the bad son. The son that was always in trouble, but Jake was the one in trouble and they just ignored it. They did not want to admit to themselves that Jake was an alcoholic. I should have done more to help him." He looked at her with tears streaming down his face. "They told me once that they wished it had been me that had been killed. And so do I."

Jessica continued to rubbed his back in a gentle circular motion. She had never met her in-laws and had always wondered why. Travis had never talked about them. Now she knew why. She felt her eyes fill with sympathetic tears. Her parents had always played a big role in her life and could not imagine life without them. She could not imagine what Travis had lived with. Being accused of killing his brother was a horrible burden for him. "I am so sorry, Travis," she told him.

Travis leaned against the wall both physically and mentally exhausted. He closed his eyes and ran his hands over his face. "I wish it had been me in the car instead of him."

Jessica felt her heart break for him. But now a lot of things made sense to her. Maybe now he would let her help him. "Come on," she said, putting an arm around his waist. "Lets go home."

Chapter Twelve

The next morning Jessica checked on Travis. She opened the door to the guest bedroom and saw him sitting in the chair next to the window. He was holding a pillow tightly to his chest. Travis was still dressed in the khaki pants and blue shirt from yesterday. He stared blankly out the window. Travis ignored her as she came into the room. She walked over to him and sat down on the bed. Jessica looked at him with concern. "Travis?" she asked, touching his arm gently. "Travis, are you okay?"

He looked over at her. His blue eyes were rimmed red. Travis looked like he had been up all night. "Morning, Jessica."

Jessica was worried about him. "How are you? Did you get any sleep last night?" She had finally fell asleep about one that morning. Before that she had tossed and turned a majority of the night.

"No, I didn't. I couldn't sleep at all," he admitted to her. "Every time I closed my eyes all I could see was Jack's car on fire." He leaned over and put his forehead in the palms of his hands. "I miss him so much, Jessie."

Jessica put her arms around him and hugged him. "You have had this bottled up inside for so long."

"It hurt to much to talk about it." He looked over at her with tears in his eyes. "Even to you." Travis got up and tossed the pillow on the bed. He began to walk around the room. "When Abby started drinking all I could think was not again."

"I understand."

Travis looked over at her and shook his head. "No, you don't. You have never lost someone you love to alcohol."

Jessica met his eyes. "No, I haven't. Thank God." She went over to where he was standing and took his hands in hers and winced as she felt how cold they were. "You have pushed me away because of this. You should have talked to me. I could have helped you."

Travis saw the sincerity in her eyes. He knew that she was telling him the truth. He had shut her and Abby out. And then he had accused them of shutting *him* out of their lives. "I am sorry, Jessica. I should have told you. I just thought that you would think it was my fault, too. I thought you would have hated me, too," he looked away from her.

"I could never hate you," she made him look at her. "Travis, it was an accident. It was a horrible, tragic accident. But it was not your fault. Your brother knew he shouldn't have been driving that night, but he did." She squeezed his hands tightly. "If he were here now he would not want you to blame yourself."

Travis grasped her hands just as tightly. Maybe she was right. Maybe he should let go of his guilt. "I want to believe you. But it's hard." He let them go and turned to face the window again. "It was easy for me to shut down when Abby began to drink. I could not stand the thought of losing Abby like I did Jack. It was so easy to throw myself into my work so I would not have to deal with her."

141

"I think you should be telling that to Abby," Jessica said, touching his shoulder. "She needs to hear that."

Travis nodded. She was right. He did need to tell Abby. He had to make her understand. "I am going to go tell her now, while I have still have the nerve to do it." He headed toward the door. Jessica was right behind him. He glanced over his shoulder at her. "I have to do this by myself."

Jessica understood. He needed to talk to Abby alone. They need to work things out on their own. If they needed her they would call for her. She gave him an encouraging smile as he left the room.

Travis gathered his courage and knocked on Abby's bedroom door. He did not know how this was going to work out. "Come in," he heard her call out. He took in another deep breath and went in. Abby looked up from the computer. She was not happy to see him. She had hoped to avoid him. "What is it?"

Travis entered the room and sat down on the unmade bed. "Abby, we need to talk."

Abby sighed and hit the 'save' button on her computer. She pivoted around in her chair to face him. She met her father's troubled gaze. "What is this about?"

"I want to tell you about your Uncle Jack."

Abby was confused. "I don't have an uncle, do I?" She titled her head.

Travis rubbed his face with his hands and prayed that he would not break down. "Yes, you do. Well, you did," he looked at her. "He was killed in a drunk drive accident when he was eighteen."

Abby was stunned. "I am sorry," was all she could think of to say. She thought back to what Melissa had told her about her younger sister.

Travis reached over and took her hands. "I was scared, Abby. I could not stand the thought that I could lose you like I lost my brother." He stopped talking and blinked back the tears that threatened him. He did not want to start crying. "I am sorry that my fear made you think that I was ashamed of you. That is the farthest thing from the truth. I am very proud of you." Travis pulled her close to him and held her. He gave her a kiss on her temple. "To tell the truth I am ashamed of the way I have treated you the last several months. I have not been the father you needed."

Abby hugged him back. "I am sorry about your brother." She pulled back and gave him a wobbly smile. "And I am sorry for everything that I have put you through. I have not been the best daughter either."

"Thanks." He reluctantly let go of his daughter. He smiled at her and brushed her hair out of her face. "I have so many regrets. I should have been more supportive to you. But I promise you that from now on I am going to be your biggest champion."

Abby laughed, "Thanks, Dad."

Travis made her look at him. "I am telling you the truth, Abby." He put a hand on her cheek. "I am going to be on your side." He pulled her into another hug. "I want you to remember that no matter what, I love you."

"I love you too, Dad."

Travis felt his heart lighten. His daughter loved him again. He wished he could stay in this moment forever. But he knew that he could not. Especially if he continued with his campaign. He released Abby. "I better let you get back to work. What are you doing? Homework?"

Jessica giggled again, "Dad, I am on summer vacation. I am working on a book. I want to see if I can get it published."

Travis gave a sad smile as he thought back to his past. "Your Uncle Jack was a good writer. He used to write short stories and poems all the time. I still have some of them. I'll have to show them to you sometime," Travis looked at Abby and beamed with pride. "My daughter the author. I could live with that." He got up from the bed. Travis left the room and ran into Jessica.

"How did it go?" she wanted to know.

"We are well on the road to reconciliation." Travis hugged Jessica happily. Travis knew things were not perfect between him and Abby, but it was a start.

Jessica pulled away from her husband. "I am thrilled that you and Abby are working out your problems." She readjusted her blouse and pushed her hair out of her face.

Travis put his hands on her arms. "There is something I need to do."

"What's that?"

"I need to go to Montana for a few days. There is someone I need to see," he told her. "I should have done this a long time ago."

Jessica realized what he was going to do. "I understand. Do you want me to go with you?"

Travis shook his head. "No, I have to do this alone." He looked at his wife hopefully. "Can I call you while I am gone?"

"Yes, you can. I'll be here if you need me," she promised him.

* * * * * * * * * * *

Later, that afternoon, Travis landed in Montana. He was thrilled that he had been able to get a flight so soon. He collected his suitcase and walked over to the car rental desk. Once he had rented a small compact car he headed to the cemetery where Jack was buried. Travis parked his car in the parking lot and walked through the gate. He stopped at the cemetery's caretaker's house and got directions to his brother's grave. He made his way through the small private cemetery till he found a medium sized black marble marker. Travis read the marker:

Beloved Son, Brother, and Friend
Jack Moore
1962-1980

Travis knelt down and laid the flowers down that he had brought. "Hi, big brother. Sorry, I have not been to see you sooner. I don't have any real good excuse why I haven't." He touched the lettering lightly. "I miss you, Jack. I have missed you so much. There have been times when I have needed my big brother. Why did you have to leave me?" Tears rolled down his cheeks, but he did not care. He let them fall down and land on his legs. "We should never have been drinking. I should have stopped you from drinking and driving that night." He leaned his head back. "I knew you were in trouble, but I did nothing. I should have done something to help you. I failed you in the worse possible way. And for that I am sorry. I am so sorry. I would give anything to have you back." He broke down. Travis hugged the cold marble tombstone like he was hugging Jack. Travis did not care if anyone saw him.

After a few minutes Travis was able to calm down. He let go of the marker. He sat back on his heels and wiped his eyes with the back of his hands. "I got married, Jack. I married a beautiful, smart, wonderful, woman named Jessica Smith. We have a beautiful daughter named Abby. She is going to be a writer like you. The two of you would have gotten a long greatly." Travis stopped. He was afraid

145

he was going to break down again, but he could not. He had to tell Jack about his life. "Abby had some of rough times, but she is doing better now. I am very proud of Abby. Jessica has been a rock through all this. I love her," Travis smiled sadly and continued on, "Jessica and I are going to have another child. And I could not be happier." He looked up at the clear blue sky. "I don't know who I am anymore, Jack. I thought I wanted to be president, but I don't know anymore." Travis looked over at the majestic mountains. "I don't even know if I want to be in politics anymore," he admitted. Travis was stunned at the omission that he had just made. But he did feel like a weight had been lifted from his shoulders.

Travis felt better than he had in years. He looked at the tombstone and touched it again gently. It felt like Jack had been listening to him the whole time he had been talking. "I love you, Jack. I'll be back soon to visit." He headed back to his car.

* * * * * * * * * * * *

Two days later, Travis returned to Washington D.C. The first thing he wanted to do was see Jessica. He arrived at the house just as Abby and Melissa where leaving for an A.A meeting. He said hello to both of them and went into the house. Jessica was sitting in the chair reading a book when he came into the living room. "Travis, welcome home! How did it go?"

Travis sat down on the couch and gave her a huge smile. "It went well," he told her. He did not want to go in to the details. He was not ready for that. But there was something weighing on his mind that he had to tell her. "Jessica, I need to make some life changes."

Jessica felt her heart drop down to her stomach when she heard the tone of his voice. *He is going to continue his run for president. I know he is,* she thought with dread. "What?"

"I wish I could explain it better, but I can't," he said. Travis saw the confusion in her eyes. "I just need time to think. I need time to myself. I am just not happy where my life is right now." He reached over and took her hand and squeezed it. "But I do know I want you in my life."

Jessica returned the squeeze. She was not entirely sure of what he was trying to say. "Do what you have to do. And when you are ready, I'll be waiting for you."

* * * * * * * * * * * *

At nine months pregnant, Jessica did not feel like doing a whole lot. She was two weeks over due and she was miserable. Her back had been hurting since she had woken up that morning. She laid on her bed with a heating pad on her back. To her dismay it was not working. She let out a moan and rubbed her huge stomach. The phone rang and she picked up the phone cordless that was beside her. "Hello?" she asked.

"Jessica, it's Travis."

Despite how bad she was feeling she smiled. Hearing Travis's voice always made her feel better. Jessica sat up a little. "What's going on, Travis?"

"I need to see you. Can I come over in an hour?" he wanted to know.

"Sure. Abby and I'll be here."

"Great, I'll see you then," he said and hung up.

Jessica sighed and hit the disconnect button on her phone and dropped it back down on the bed. She struggled to sit up. *Maybe that will help my back,* Jessica thought hopefully.

"Mom!" Abby said, as she came into the room. "Let me help you." She helped her mother sit up on the side of the bed. "Is that better?"

Jessica nodded even though it was not. "I better help you put the finishing touches on the nursery." With Abby's help she stood up.

"Don't worry about it, Mom. I just finished it. I want you to come see it." She saw the pained look on her mother's face and felt her heart constrict. "Mom, are you alright?"

"For a fat cow, I am great," Jessica joked. She rubbed her lower back and grimaced.

"Mom, you are not a fat cow."

Jessica looked over at Abby. "Ever since I lost sight of my feet I have known that I was a whale." She opened the door to the nursery and went in. Jessica was thrilled by what she saw. Abby had also painted the walls a mint green. She had finished putting the Winnie the Pooh characters on the wall. The crib was next to the wall by the window. It had a mobile hanging over it with Tigger, Piglet, and Winnie hanging from it. Painted on the far wall was Christopher Robin. Over his head was a banner that read, 'Welcome to the Hundred-Acre Woods.' The baby's clothes where now in the dresser and not stacked on the changing table.

"What do you think?" Abby asked anxiously. She held her breath as her mother looked around the room.

Jessica glanced over at Abby and gave her a happy smile. She gave Abby a grateful hug. "Thank you, Abby. But you did not have to do this. I could have finished it."

"I wanted to do this for you, Mom. I really enjoyed it."

Jessica continued to look around the room. "When your father arrives we'll have to show it to him. He'll love it, too." She went over to the crib and touched the mobile and straightened the yellow comforter.

Abby felt her pride grow. She was pleased that Jessica liked the room and hoped that Travis would like it just as much. She and Travis had been getting along better. He had attended several Parents with Alcoholic Children meetings with Jessica. And he got more involved with Abby's recovery. The two of them attended several counseling sessions. Plus, he had stared a teen outreach program to help under privileged teenagers. It gave teenagers a safe place to go after school. They could play sports, work on the computer, or receive tutoring. It was a place that would give them the help they might not receive otherwise. It also provided family counseling sessions. Abby and her mother had been involved with the project from the beginning. "Why is Dad coming over for?"

"He said he just wants to talk. Probably, something about the Outreach Program."

Abby eyed her mother. She looked pale and her hair was disheveled. "You need to put on some make-up and brush your hair," she suggested. Abby wanted her mother to look her best when her father saw her.

Jessica laughed, "That's a gentle hint." She headed for the door.

"I am glad you like the nursery."

Jessica smiled at her over her shoulder and went into her room. She walked over to her dresser and looked in the mirror. *Ugh. Abby was right I look awful,* she thought, staring at her reflection. Jessica picked up the brush and ran it through her auburn hair. Suddenly a sharp pain shot through abdomen. She doubled over and clutched her stomach. She whimpered. The pain was horrendous. Even more than the false labor pains she had a few months ago.

149

"Abby," was all she could whisper. The pain eased some. "Abby!" she yelled.

Abby ran into the bedroom and saw what condition her mother was in. She knew immediately that Jessica was in labor. Abby hurried to her mother's side. "We got to get you to the hospital."

Abby helped her mother down the stairs and into the living room. Jessica told her that she need to sit down. Abby helped sit down on the couch. Jessica did her Lamaze breathing and tried not to panic. "Go bring the car around."

Abby was grateful for something to do. She ran out to bring the car around to the front of the house. Just as she was opening the front door her father walked up. She was never happier to see him. Travis was concerned when he saw Abby's panic stricken face. "Abby, what is going on?"

"Mom's in labor," she said, rushing past him. "She wants me to get the car."

Travis went pale. "Hurry," he ordered. Travis rushed into the living room. He knelt down in front of Jessica. His heart stopped when he saw her face. Jessica's face was bathed in sweat and tears. "Jessie." He took out his handkerchief and gently wiped her face.

Jessica looked at him and burst into loud sobs. She held out her arms to him. Travis sat down next to her and pulled her into a hug. She buried her face in his shoulder. "It hurts, Travis. It really, really, hurts," she cried. "It was not like this with Abby."

Travis smoothed her hair back. "You are doing great. Everything is going to be fine," he said encouragingly. "Before you know it we are going to have a baby." He felt her grip the back of his shirt. "Breathe. Come on, Jessica, breathe." He commanded when he realized she was having another contraction.

Jessica huffed and puffed as she had been taught in Lamaze class. She thought the worse was over when her water broke. She leaned against his chest. "My water broke. I don't think I can make to the hospital. What are we going to do?"

Travis felt his panic grow. He tried to give her a reassuring smile. Mentally, he was freaking out. "Everything is going to be fine. You and the baby will be alright. You are going to have to trust me." He helped her lay back on the couch. Travis placed two pillows behind her back.

"Dad, what's going on?" Abby asked, coming back into the living room. She looked over at her mom. "Dad?" she asked again.

Travis looked quickly at Abby and then back at Jessica who was obviously having another labor pain. "Your mom is going to have the baby here. I need you to get me a couple of towels." He pulled the blue afghan off the chair and put it over Jessica's knees. "Hurry." He rolled up the sleeves of his red shirt.

Abby hurried to get the towels that he asked for. Jessica looked up at Travis with fear in her eyes. "I am scared. It's happening so fast." She felt another sever pain go through her and she cried. "Travis, it's not going to be much longer."

Travis nodded. She did not need to tell him twice. "You can do this."

"The baby is going to be okay, isn't it?" She felt a contraction. Jessica clutched her stomach and screamed. "I can't do this." She rolled her head back and forth on the pillow. Jessica felt a cold cloth on her forehead. She opened her eyes and saw Abby. Jessica reached out a hand to Abby and she grasped it. "Promise me," she said to both of them. "Promise me that if anything goes wrong, you'll save my baby. I don't care what happens to me just save the baby."

"You and the baby are going to be fine," Travis said, with a stubborn look in his eyes. "I am not going to lose either of you."

Jessica felt a little bit better. Then she was hit with an urge to push. She did not even have time to tell Travis. She pushed as hard as she could. "Good job, Jessica. Keep it up," Travis said.

"I don't want to have my baby on the couch," Jessica cried. "I want to have my baby in the hospital."

"Jessica, you don't have much of a choice," Travis said. "Because, it is coming now. I see the top of the head."

Jessica pushed again and rested against the pillows. Abby wiped the sweat of her mother's face, but it did not do much good. Beads of sweat reappeared instantly. "Mom, you are doing great."

Jessica pushed again. "Push one more time, Jessica. Just once more and then you can hold your baby," Travis promised. Jessica moaned in agony. "The baby is almost here."

Jessica nodded and pushed with the last of her strength. She collapsed back on to the couch.

"You are going to have to push again," Travis told her.

"I can't!" Jessica cried. "You told me I just had to push one more time. I can't push again. It's too hard." She felt another contraction coming. "I want to die!" She screamed. Jessica looked over at Abby with pleading eyes. "Help me," she begged her.

Abby leaned closer to her mother and whispered in her ear. "Come on, Mom. You can do this." She brushed Jessica's sweaty hair out of her face. Abby could not believe how calm she was acting because she did not feel calm inside.

Travis made Jessica look at him. "Jessica, you are one the strongest and bravest women I have ever known. You can deliver this baby. I know you can. Now push!"

Jessica sat up and pushed. She heard a small wail and it grew louder. "Travis..." she said weakly. "My baby..."

Travis looked at her with huge smile on his face. "It's a boy. We have a son." He gently cleaned the screaming baby. Travis cuddled his son in his arms for a few minutes before handing him to his mother.

Jessica took the baby from her husband. She kissed him tenderly on the forehead. Tears of joy were streaming down her face. "He's beautiful," she said, giving her son a loving smile. Jessica maneuvered over so Abby could have a better look at her new brother. Abby stroked the baby's plump cheek with her finger. "Absolutely beautiful."

* * * * * * * * * * * *

Later, that night Jessica was sitting in her hospital bed holding the baby. She had just finished feeding him and he was about to fall asleep. She adjusted herself so she could be more comfortable without disturbing the baby. She wondered where Abby and Travis had gone. Just then Travis came into her room carrying a gigantic black teddy bear with a red ribbon around its neck. "Who's bear is that supposed to be?" she asked, with a laugh.

Travis sat it down in the chair. "Well, if he is good I'll be willing to share it with him." He reached into his pants pocket and pulled out a small box. "I have something for his mother as well." He handed it to her.

"Can you take the baby so I can what you got me?" Travis took their son from her and she opened the box. Inside laid a beautiful gold ring with the birthstones of their children. The diamond for Abby's birthday and a sapphire for their new son. "Its gorgeous," she told him. Jessica slipped it on to her finger.

Travis looked at her with a pleased look on his face. "I am glad you like it." He handed the baby back to his mother. Travis gave Jessica a gentle kiss on the lips. "I love you, Jessica."

She kissed him back. "I love you too, Travis."

He stroked her cheek. "Your beautiful."

Jessica could not help but giggle, "I just gave birth to a baby. My hair is a mess, I have no make-up on, and I am in a hospital gown. If this is your idea of beautiful, you have a very warped since of beauty."

"You beautiful to me," he repeated to her.

Jessica gave an embarrassed smile and looked down at her sleeping son in her arms. They had more important things to discuss than how she looked. "I have been thinking about names."

"Did you come up with anything?"

Jessica not sure how he would feel about her suggestion, but she decided to make it anyway. "One name keeps coming to mind, but I am not sure how you will feel about it."

Travis looked at her curiously. "What is it?"

"Jack."

Travis looked at her with surprise. "You would name him after my brother?"

"Yes. So what do you think?"

Travis was thrilled. He had been thinking about suggesting that they name him after his brother as well.

"Thank you, Jessica. That means a lot to me." He picked up the teddy bear and sat it on the floor. He sat down in the chair and gave Jessica a serious look. "There is something I have to tell you. It's about the election."

Oh, no not that, she thought. Jessica did not meet her husband's gaze. *Why does he have to talk about the election? Today of all days?* "What about it?"

Travis took a deep breath. "I have decided to drop out of the race for president," He held a hand up to keep her from interrupting him. "I thought running for president would make me happy. But it hasn't." He leaned closer to the bed. "I also resigned from the senate."

"Why?"

"Same reason," he admitted. "I have not been happy for a long time. I thought throwing myself into my career would make me feel better about myself, but it didn't. I always thought that I wanted a career in politics, but this year has made me think otherwise." Travis gave a smile that made him look twenty years younger. "What has made me happy is working with these kids who are in trouble. Yesterday two kids told me that they got scholarships to college. One said that he never thought he would be able to go."

"That's great," Jessica said, feeling happy for him. Travis did look happier than she had seen him in a long time. "What will you do now?"

"I am going to continue to work at the Outreach Center. And I am planning on opening others as well." He reached over and touched one Jake's little hands. "There are a lot of kids that need help. If I can make a difference in these kid's lives, then I should do it. Abby even agreed to help me."

155

Jessica was thrilled that Travis and Abby had worked through their issues and were now going to helping others. "Oh, Travis, that's wonderful." She could not help but wonder where she fit in to his new life.

Travis seemed to be reading her mind. He got up and sat on the bed next to her. He put an arm around her and pulled her close to him. "Can I come home? I know that I don't deserve another chance. But will you give me one? Can we be a family again?" he chocked out.

Tears spilled down her cheeks. It was more than she had hoped for. She had been praying for this day for a long time. She laid her head on his chest and he stroked her hair. "This is what I want. I want us to be a family again." She lifted her head and Travis gave her a passionate kiss.

Abby came into the room at that moment. She watched them for a minute wondering if she should leave and give them their privacy. Travis saw her standing there and gave her a smile. He held his arm to her for her to join them. Abby went over to the bed and joined them in the group hug.

Travis held his family tightly. He could not remember the last time he had been so happy.

Political Family

Thorman

Authorhouse

Cono

②

10.95

HT-2

Oxf. Dict. of Classical Myth + Religion

Price Nov

Oxford 019-280288-7

39.95 Hc

10

About the Author

Heather Thoroman lives in a small town in southern Indiana. Political Family is Heather's first book to be published. She is currently working on her second entitled, 10:15. While attending Oakland City University, Bedford, she won literature contests. Heather has a bachelor degree in Social Science.

Printed in the United States
24393LVS00001B/88-114

9 781420 804386